Lightning and Insight

BY SUSAN D WATSON

DORRANCE
PUBLISHING CO
EST. 1920
PITTSBURGH, PENNSYLVANIA 15238

Dorrance Publishing Co
585 Alpha Drive
Pittsburgh, PA 15238
Visit our website at *www.dorrancebookstore.com*

ISBN: 979-8-8860-4423-2
eISBN: 979-8-8868-3844-2

LIGHTNING AND INSIGHT

Lightning Begins

Alonzo called out to his son, Jacob, "Do you have the produce set up? The kitchenware? The other items, are they set up for sale?"

Both William and Jacob looked up. "Yes, we're ready. Do you want us to go hunt the items we need?" asked Jacob.

"Yes, but don't buy or trade for anything. If you find books, that would be good, too, but everything else comes first. Do you have the list?"

"Yes!" Both boys were excited to be at this marketplace, hoping to find items that might make them money as well as entertain them through the winter.

"Then go ahead, be back before the sun hits midmorning," said Alonzo.

Alonzo and his two boys were selling farm produce, trinkets, and kitchenware they had spent the winter making for sale. They bought and frequently traded for items they thought would need in the future, too. The boys, Jacob and William, were having a great time, and occasionally would charm their customers or other vendors into giving them small items. Alonzo was not quite sure if he should be proud of that talent or embarrassed. One smile, a song, or a cute story from one boy or the other brought him more profit, so it was hard to leave them home with their mother.

Th older boy, Jacob, was good at telling stories and collecting them, especially about magic and wizardry. The younger boy, William could hear any piece of music and sing it as a song, creating his own lyrics if necessary. Then Jacob would merely hold the coins for someone who truly needed an item but was short on money.

William and Jacob checked each stall for books, of course, but also checked for items on their list. Each time they found an item on their list, they negotiated for a good price and for delivery to their father's wagon. It was going very well for them on this trip. Working on their sales skills, they also checked each stall for items the seller might need.

At the last stall, William called out, "Jacob! Come look at this box of books!"

Inside were books on farming, gardening, music, legends, and general history. The boys dug through about half the books and decided they would be saleable. At that moment Jacob felt a nip on a finger and snatched his hand back out.

"Something in this box of books bit me! Do you store mice here?" Jacob exclaimed.

William reached in and moved a few books aside, certain there would be a mouse or something like that in the box.

"Yipes! I've been nipped, too! There has to be a mouse in there!"

The storekeeper sighed and came over to check, picking books out and stacking them aside. "I don't see a mouse, just books. Do you want the box of books?"

"I know I was bitten but let me look at them and pack them back into box," said Jacob.

"These books are clean of mouse poop and are in reasonable shape," the shopkeeper said, as he helped the boys pack the books into the box.

"Well, it might have been anything, a sliver or who knows what. I'm going to ask my father to look at this box of books. Perhaps he'll want it," said William.

"I'll give him a discount on the box, if he takes it, for your trouble," stated the shopkeeper.

Later, the shopkeeper walked through the market and saw the boys making money on their own, William singing and Jacob telling stories of magic and adventure. He stopped and watched for a while and when Alonzo showed up, he introduced himself. After a little bartering, the bookseller traded the box of books for several items. Both gentlemen were pleased with the bargain and parted ways.

Alonzo had traveled far from home and at this point decided to head back home. Usually, they traveled longer but their profits were up as well as luck.

They packed up the wagon, harnessed the horses started homeward. Jacob and William looked in the back of the wagon and found the box that had bitten them. Nothing seemed amiss, so each evening Alonzo would pick up a story book and read from it. The stories were about adventure and magic and the boys really enjoyed them. When they had spare time, the boys would act out some of the stories with startling clarity. Alonzo began to wonder if the boys had picked a stray talent from an ancestor.

As days passed, Alonzo noticed the boys were far more mature than they should be for their age. At first Alonzo decided that the boys were just growing up due to the journey and the sales they worked at. Then he watched them act out adventures and scenes from the books, it all seemed more real than it used to be. When William would sing, his songs were far more persuasive ever before and Jacob was writing out spells that worked. Alonzo began to check the books in the box and read them before he handed them to the boys. He couldn't find a reason for the change.

The last leg of their journey to home went through an area known for legends of dragons. Out of the grassy plains through woods and forests, the finally found their way up a legendary pass. At the top of the pass, Alonzo had to stop and rest the horses in a wide spot. He wasn't going to let the boys stray from the wagon, so he told them to get a book. As they did so, one book nobody noticed before fell out of the box and out of the wagon. The book's pages fluttered open and closed a few times before it came to a stop. Alonzo was sure he saw a glittering light from the pages as they moved. The boys went to retrieve it when Alonzo told them to stop. He explained the area they were in was known for magic of all kinds, dragons and many other mysteries and it was time for a lot of caution. Alonzo pulled the boys away from the book and went to look at it and could see it was a grimoire. The glittering light around the grimoire meant a wizard was trapped in it. Alonzo told the boys someone was attached to the book, likely a wizard who wanted out, possibly being tortured by the book.

Jacob muttered "That's a bad thing," to William.

When Alonzo turned back to the book, he saw the pages flipping one way and then the other, back and forth. Alonzo immediately pulled out a small leather pouch and threw a handful of the contents on the book. The book exploded into flames and as it burned to ash, the book screamed. Jacob grabbed the leather pouch and threw more of the contents on the book. A wind blew the ashes away. The boys were shaken but Alonzo grabbed them and made them get into the wagon. He asked the boys if they knew their way home from there and both boys nodded. Alonzo looked relieved until a sudden wind picked up and seemed to snatch Alonzo away, leaving the wagon. In the distance, the boys could hear an angry roar. Both boys were terrified but the horses began to pull the wagon down the road as if nothing had happened. Looking up, the boys could see a large, winged creature flying in the distance and later another following it.

Shaken, the boys agreed to keep the flying creatures secret. Those objects were large enough to be dragons and since the area was known for dragons they certainly didn't want to offend them.

⚡

A YOUNG WOMAN SAT INSIDE HER CABIN, RESTING AFTER WEEKS of taking care of the little plot of land she and her family had lived on for generations. In the morning, she took the milk cow and the horse out to pasture, worked her spring garden, hunted for the eggs her chickens had laid, and many other chores. In the evening, after she had returned the animals to the barn, she made her meal and mended clothing, and she sat for a while. Her husband and two sons were days late returning from market.

Louiza stood up from the chair and felt her baby moving inside. Holding her hand on her belly, she went outside to the barn, and patted the horses and the cow one more time. Good night to the animals had been a ritual for her since she was a small child herself, and she cherished such moments. Outside, she heard someone pounding on the front door of cottage.

Louiza walked out of the back of little barn and peered at the cottage. A large man was standing in front of the cottage, pacing. He went back to the door and knocked again, more politely. He called out "Louiza! Are you there?" After a few more moments, he just lifted the handle and walked into the cottage.

Louiza walked to the door and peered in. The fellow had simply sat down in her husband's chair and watched the fireplace as if there flames in it. Louiza walked in the door and inquired "What do you want?"

The man was startled and replied, "I met your husband and boys at the market. I was sent here."

"When will they be back?"

"I don't know. Your husband wanted me to give you something. I wanted to talk to him further, but when I went back, he and the boys were gone. I've known him for years." He handed her a small leather packet.

Breaking the wax seal and opening up the packet, she found a few gems and a note. The note told her to sell everything to man that delivered the note and leave. Startled, she nearly dropped the packet. The small farm had been in her family for generations. She stood up and made another cup of tea and handed it to her visitor.

"My husband gave this to you?"

"Yes. He said it important that I got it to you right away. Thank you for the tea, I haven't stopped for anything since they disappeared."

"It says that I am to sell you everything and leave."

He looked genuinely shocked. "I have the means to do so, and I could probably put a one of my serfs here. Your husband has been of value for years, but this is disturbing. Where will you go?"

"I'm not sure, but I know of several places where I'd be welcome. I have horses and a cart, but this notes says everything. Perhaps if I just took one horse…"

"Look further. I was told there was a map in there."

Louiza picked up the packet and went into the small kitchen. She carefully spread the packet and the note out on the table near the small kitchen woodstove and smoothed both out very flat. She took the gems into her hand and held them tightly while she stared at the parchment. Finally, she wiped it gently and put the gems on it. The warmth of the stove caused a map to appear. There were several symbols on the inside of the packet, which look like a chair and a table. As she moved the smooth gems over each symbol another trail appeared through an area her husband used to describe to her long ago. She smiled and felt the baby moving again. The baby is young, but she would have to get there soon.

Standing up, she picked up the packet. "I know the place, but I've never been there. Can you just put a serf here? There's only so much money I can carry without endangering myself." Stepping aside, she sorts and packs things out for the trip.

"Besides," Louiza continued, "women can't own or sell property. If a man isn't present here, someone will just take it anyway. If I make any kind of exchange with you, I couldn't come back," she added.

Embarrassed, the man looked aside. After a moment, he asked "How long before you'll gone."

"I'm about to leave. I almost have enough together to begin this journey." She looked at him briefly and saw his embarrassment. "You look more honest than most who would have done this."

He helped her with her baggage and took it out to the small barn. She hooked up one horse to the cart and a put small saddle on the other horse, while the baggage went into the cart and Louiza covered it with hay. The fellow helps her put a covering goes over the hay. Smiling, she leaves the place behind. The man stood outside watching her go, in apparent shock. Finally, he shuts up the barn and house, checks the rest the property and goes his way, deciding which serf will take care of the property and how to make it profitable. It's what he does.

Riding the horse, with a saddle bag stuffed with a seemingly random assortment of items, Louiza took heart in this new adventure. Her clothes are neatly packed, the inexpensive gems in a hidden pocket and the map became part of her belt, looking like a simple bit of leather. The horse and cart follow her with good will. Soon, Louiza moves off the main road, taking a branch to her destination. The trees crowd the path, the sun will set soon, so Louiza looks for a campsite. Looking through the woods, she sees what looks like a track that will allow both horses and the cart to pass through.

When she followed the track, she clearly saw people were using the track, just as she. Curious, she tried to not look around her. Instead, she left her eyes slightly unfocused and paid attention. Others like her were camping off to one side or the other, and she selected a site. Slowing her horse down, she followed that track.

Louiza greeted that group ahead of time, she found a spot nearby and dismounted. A few women come up and quietly her helped her. One of them lead her horse farther into the woods and indicates she should follow to a place that will hide her and her horses as swell as a small fire. Louiza nodded her head, and the woman indicates the need for silence.

That night, Louiza slept in the cart with the horses staying nearby. In the morning, the women disappeared. The horses were calmly grazing, so Louiza eats, too. Again, she checked the map and notes and discovers she had taken a short cut. Tucking the map away, Louiza tidies up the campsite. It's hard to hide the tracks of her passage.

The travel to her destination is gratefully boring, so she often picks up a lone woman going the same way and gives her a ride. The women rarely stay long, and say little, but they are homeless, too. Their husbands disappeared, their homes taken and most of them are looking for relatives to take them in. The thinner ones, she'd find a snack, eggs, or something for them to eat.

Eventually, Louiza finds the last branch she must take to her husband's birthplace. Her food is running low and one morning she finds someone put food in her cart. Smiling, she eats and walks with the horses. Eventually, the road narrows so much she must guide the lead horse down a barely visible track. Passing through a gap in the trees, Louiza finds the property, and brings the horses and wagon along. Sighing, takes the horses to the barn, unhooks them and leads them out to an unfenced pasture.

Walking around the place, she can clearly see that nobody has been there for a long time. The place is in need of many minor repairs and there's nothing anywhere to indicate any one has lived there for years. Fortunately, the roof of each the structures appear intact but any paint on the buildings had faded long ago.

Picking up her possessions, she walks into the house. It's dusty but otherwise intact. With the baby getting more active, Louiza is sure she'll deliver the baby soon. In her pack, there is little food left, so Louiza searches the woods and the pasture to collect what she can for her meals.

That evening, as Louiza is about to fall asleep on a bedroll, she hears one horse snort then the other one. Quickly she goes out to the barn. The horses have settled down, and everything seems fine when someone shifts in the loft. She calls out, "Who is there? Why are you hiding?"

Two woman come down from the loft and look at the ground, embarrassed. Louiza recognizes them from the trail, and asks "Do you need help?"

One looks up hopefully and says, "We needed help and you're the only one who tried. Can we stay? We can see this property has been stripped as was ours. We've heard there's a community of women like us nearby, but we haven't found it."

"Yes, you can stay for now. My husband sent me out here, knowing my property was going to be taken. I'm sure he will be out here when he can."

"Your baby is due soon. Many of us have nowhere to go. At least we'd be as safe here than by ourselves in the woods."

"We'll sort this out in the morning." Louiza nodded and said, "Make yourself comfortable for the night."

The two women crawled back up into the loft, "Good night, indeed. Thank you."

In the morning, Louiza got up and went out to look for more food. There was a bucket of water near the from door. A water barrel looked as if someone was trying to repair it. The horses were back in the pasture. And there were easily over a dozen women walking in and out of the woods, conferring with each other, bringing what they could find for firewood, food and more. A few that looked like they were trying to assemble furniture and weapons and were startled to see Louiza.

Louiza merely smiled and greeted them. "Good morning. How many of you are out there?"

One, clearly embarrassed, spoke up, "Over thirty of us, so far, and many are comfortable in the wilds."

"Well," said Louiza, "It seems that you are determined to be here and willing to do what you feel is necessary. I'm not going to complain. But I do find it odd so many women are homeless suddenly. There are absolutely no supplies here, and it's been vacant a long time. I have a few rooms in the house that are vacant and that's it.'

"Some have been in the woods a long time and are used to it. Others are finding their way. We're here to return the help you gave on the trail." The woman nodded at Louiza's belly. "You'll need help soon, and some of us are good with birthing." The woman paused and took a breath, saying "Many of us have had our infants and children stolen, so at a certain point, you may want to be somewhere else."

Louiza gathered her wits for a moment, looking at the weapons they were trying to assemble. "I understand. Set yourselves up as you need to and if I find anything we can use or anywhere we can go, I need to know how to contact someone."

"Someone will be here. We're tired and we are doing everything we can to keep our children. You aren't going to be alone."

Louiza thanked her and went into the woods to forage. When she came back she couldn't see any evidence of anyone nearby. She entered the house, finding a small pile of firewood stacked neatly for her cooking use. A note on the table said that Louiza would have a few boarders soon, willing to work for staying in the house.

The boarders showed up and stayed, doing more chores as Louiza's pregnancy advanced. Some stayed several days, others only overnight but Louiza was never left alone. One day an unfamiliar woman showed up at the door. A couple of the boarders were standing with Louiza and lit up with delight. One spoke up and said, "She's here to stay a while as we think you're about to deliver."

When inside, the woman merely asked to touch her belly. As she put her hand towards Louiza's belly, a small spark jumped to the woman's hand. Startled, the woman jumped back. "Well, that's different." The woman tried again, and the spark was a little brighter and floated in the air before it dissipated. "That's better. It's what I expected a generation ago. Your husband's family skipped a generation, too. You'll have a lot of help in raising this one, and there are kids just like this one, hiding in the woods."

Louiza smiled, remembering the kids in the woods. They looked both wild and wise. "Is it best for them to be out in the woods?"

The woman held out her hand and said, "My name is Mille. Some call me Aunt Mille." Louiza carefully shook the woman's hand.

"It's pretty simple. Too many children disappear if not closely guarded. They feel safe in the woods and there's more shelter there than you'd think. Most of them have parents actively with them, and both the parents and children are literate. We'd like to train you and your child in woodcraft, basic survival and with other skills both of you might need. In the meanwhile, I'll be here until a week or so after you deliver your child. After that, there will be someone watching over you and her, and when it is time, we will make sure you both have your share of woodcraft and other skills. It will be far easier than you think."

There was one more room left available, so Louiza guided her to the room. The woman sat down her pack. All there was in the room was a chair and a rough cot one of the visiting ladies had made. Aunt Mille sat in the chair and smiled. She closed her eyes, and the cot shimmered a little and a nice feather tick appeared on the cot. She opened her eyes, and said, "I've got everything else I need, but I need a rest. I'll be fine. Such a lovely home."

Louiza went back outside the house to do her chores. Outside was a basket full of food items as well as a skein of yarn. She looked up but nobody was around, so she took it in, unloaded the basket and found a crochet hook, so she began to make a small hood for a baby. The food would keep her, and her recent guest fed for a few days.

Each morning, another basket showed up. Occasionally, Louiza would see one of the women near the edge of the woods or the pasture with the horses. Sometimes they'd wave, other times they were busy. The barn looked clean and sturdy on the inside but rough and worn on the outside. Even the pasture looked to be growing trees around the perimeter and the house and the road in had trees enough to hide it from most travelers.

One morning, Louiza felt the pains of childbirth. Aunt Mille was at her side in a moment and two other women came in with plenty of water. Louiza was trying to put a pan on the stove, when she was guided to a nearby cot she'd not had before. The women took turns encouraging to breathe, to bear down, wiping her brow and basically keeping her from suffering alone. When the baby was delivered, they cleaned the baby and put the baby on Louiza's chest. Louiza was nearly hysterical with relief and cried, wanting her husband.

Aunt Mille said "He knows. He's glad. And he's fine."

Louiza fell asleep, holding the baby. The women carefully put the baby in its own bed next to Louiza.

Months and years passed. Emily was running in the woods and climbing trees, going into caves and coming home, to learn her letters, to read, count and all types of math. Different women would drop by to make sure Emily knew as much as they could teach. During this time, the trees and shrubs grew thickly around the property and made it difficult to find the home. Aunt Mille came back every now and then and asked Emily to play ball, which required her to create, throw and catch a small glowing ball. Essentially, Emily was having a great time.

One day, a man came through the woods to the house. He was exhausted, dirty, and smelled worse than anyone Emily had ever met. Fortunately, Emily remembered her lessons, so she ran out the back door and got her mother and a few of the other women. They asked her to bring a bucket of water, too. When Emily got to the front porch, her mother was crying and laughing at the same time.

"Emily, this is your father, Alonzo," Louiza said. "He's had a rough time and he needs a lot of help." Louiza looked up and asked for help getting him inside to wash him up.

He roused a little and said, "I shouldn't be here. I just couldn't stay away."

Louiza suddenly sobered up, saying "What happened to the boys? Were you followed?"

"We were traveling everywhere but here and shed everything we could. I was taken from them by a spelled object but was able to find out they had continued trading. I finally had to come back home. They are nearly grown and have become excellent traders. All the same, it's possible someone will find this place. This place and the woods are warded. The wards were set generations ago," he replied. "But we may have to leave, someday. People like our child are being stolen."

The nearby women stopped. Louiza nodded at one, who took off for the woods at a startling speed. Another went out to the pasture, and others spread out across the property and entered the woods from different areas. Louiza and a couple of other women brought the man inside the house and set him in a small room.

He smiled and said "I know this room. It used to be a sort of hiding space for emergencies. Bring me some food and water so I can clean myself up."

Emily stopped in the door and said "My name is Emily. I'm four years old. Mom has told me stories about you before bedtime. Will you be able to tell me stories, too?"

He laughed. "Yes. But for now, pretend I'm not here. I'm to clean up and sleep for a while. I want you to be careful about strangers. Stay as far away from them as much as you can." Emily nodded and closed the door.

Louiza brought her husband soap, water, food, and larger garments that might fit. Coming back out, she told Emily to follow her. In Louiza's room, she told Emily to hold out her hand and concentrate on the ball she could toss. Emily brought the ball into her hand. Louiza held her hand out to show her how and told Emily to float the ball above her own hand. Emily did so.

"Now, Emily, make the ball bigger. Emily slowly grew the ball to three times its size.

"Emily, this ball is basically lightning. When lightning strikes, it is a power. It can blast a tree, catch it on fire, and if it hits a human, it will hurt them. This ball, well, my mother was able to direct it to follow someone. It can kill. It also means that someone might want to take you away from here to use the lightning. And the other thing you need to know, is if you must use it, you can simply steal the lightning from the sky. I used to watch my mother do this. I'll teach you what you need to know but you'll have to be careful about where you do this."

Emily almost giggled and then realized what would happen to a tree could also happen to person or a horse. Shocked, she pulled the ball back into her hand. "Yes, mother. I'll be careful. Many of the kids have told me stories and have shown me places to hide. I can show you some more of those hiding places."

Louiza smiled and said "Thank you. That's a clever idea. Your daddy and I may need to hide."

Later that day, Louiza and Emily came back out of the woods, giggling and brushing off leaves and dirt off their clothes. Emily ran into the house and settled down near the fire. Louiza went to check on her husband and found him sleeping. She made sure to put something easy to eat near him and water.

Louiza and Emily sat near the fire, eating their own food. Emily had extracted her own promise that Louiza won't disclose the hiding places, so they talked about horses, birds, and trees they had seen. Finally, Emily went to bed and Louiza checked on her husband.

Alonzo sat up, looking weary and worn, but he had eaten and washed up. Louiza and he talked about things they used to do. He refused to tell her where he had been while missing, but only that it had been a narrow escape. Louiza did tell him she hadn't sold the property but merely left it. He smiled.

Louiza asked what happened to the boys, and he replied, "They became traders, and I hear they are doing quite well."

Days later, Alonzo had gathered enough strength to do nearly anything he wanted but wasn't sure how safe it would be for Louiza if a man suddenly appeared on her property. Louiza told him she was quite sure the nearby neighbors already knew. She explained about her journey and all the women living in the woods.

"I had wondered what happened to all those women dispossessed of their property," he said. "I heard it about it in town and sent a friend to take control of your property. When things settle down, we should be able to get it back.

Somebody had an interesting method of making money and people like us are just supposed to disappear."

"Some people disappeared quite deliberately and successfully. There are a lot of very smart children with those women in the woods. I have no idea how or where they live. When I went through the woods the first time, too many hadn't eaten for a long time. I helped and when I got here, I had more help than I hoped to have. I've exchanged garden space for products from the woods."

They talked a while and he told her he was going outside at night to exercise and check the grounds, perhaps to do chores. Later, Louiza looked out and saw him putting the horses through their paces in the pasture. A couple of women were standing at the edge of the woods watching the horses and nodding approval. After a while they went back into the woods.

Emily came out and ran towards her dad in the pasture. He picked up her and put her on the back of one of the horses. She held on tightly as her dad led the horse around the pasture once. Then he put her down, spoke to her, and she ran back to the house.

The next day, he found the tools and began repairing things here and there. A loose shingle, a board, and other small things. He had told Louiza he wanted to keep the appearance down but the utility up, so the property wouldn't attract much attention.

Days and weeks passed. Emily grew, her mom and dad kept the place up while maintaining the rundown appearance. Food was stored for the winter, and escape plans were made. There were those looking for property that would be easy to steal or sell, so more displaced people needed a place to go. The women in the woods had been slowly making homes in their caves, and others found relatives farther away they thought might accept them. Many of the older children, nearly adults, refused to leave and were creating their own homes, near and far from the woods.

Every now and again the older children would quickly visit. Several of them had decided to go on the road, trying to sell items, most handcrafted by the surrounding population. The small family made a few carvings, and Emily would often charr them slightly and rub off the excess char to help the carvings last longer. Emily's dad often brought in split lengths of soaked willow suitable for weaving. The women remaining in the woods would find low value gems to sell. These items would end up in a cart, taken by a pair of youths for sale. The fellows usually did quite well and brought back items to trade for their winter needs.

One particular autumn, two brothers came to the woods and told tales of dragons, bespelled people, spells of all kinds and more. The one called Jacob was writing a spell book while William often would sing things that entranced whomever he wanted. These two were just sprouting their beards and while they looked a bit rough from their travels, they had brought news, both good and bad. They confirmed the story of hunters looking for those with any sort of magic about them, with intent to make slaves of them.

One evening, William and Jacob came to the homestead. They were exhausted and were collecting items for their next round trip to a large city. William was a good talker, and soon Alonzo and Louiza were bringing out items to sell. Jacob would examine each item and state what he was willing to pay for it. He came to the charred carvings and stopped in shock. "Who made this?"

"Our child" said Alonzo. Jacob simply looked at him briefly and asked where the mother was.

"I am," said Louiza. Jacob looked at her and asked to see Emily.

Louiza called out like a bird and Emily came out. Jacob looked her over and very gravely introduced himself and offered to shake her hand. Emily put her hand out and when he grasped her hand he yelped and fell.

"Gribbles and Grum! You're a little glow all by yourself." Jacob stood up, laughing, brushed himself off and asked Emily to hold hands with her mother and father.

Jacob opened his book, flipping through it and slowed a few times only to continue. Finally, he cleared his throat and said "Repeat after me… 'What has been lost is now found, what has been separated is now brought together and what has been taken has been returned."

Emily felt a surge of something from her parents standing on each side of her. Startled, Alonzo and Louiza started at each other. Jacob and William were more startled when a small bolt of lightning left the family and struck the ground near the two brothers.

Jacob said, "Err… You can let go of each other. You are as you were born, the powers that were stolen are restored. Be careful, though. You'll need to watch each other as every time you use your power, someone will notice. Mine,

I can hide, as well as what I just did. Yours, well that will show. Later, perhaps I can help you hide yours.”

“Uh, Jacob, look at your hands,” William said while looking at his own.

Both William’s and Jacob’s were glowing. Louiza, Alonzo, and Emily looked at their hands, and saw the same glow. “Why do we all have glowing hands?”

“From what I’ve read, it is just a connection future, past and present,” Jacob replied.

Alonzo interrupted, “Are you two from around here?”

“No, we lost our father years ago, and have been trading and traveling since.”

“How did you lose your father?”

“It’s a bad memory,” said William. “A windstorm sang, and he left with it.”

“He was standing near an old half burned grimoire, though,” said Jacob. “I think he attacked it and escaped on the windstorm. Barely.”

“Ah,” Alonzo said. “You don’t have that old grimoire?”

“No, burned it. It stank and had something horrible attached to it. But I wrote one of my own.”

“Heard that writing your own can be dangerous. Watch out what finds yours or sees it. Apart from theft, grimoires have a life of their own.”

Jacob looked pensive for a moment and said “Pretty sure the one we burned absorbed someone and it wasn’t our father. Before he destroyed it he told us the grimoire wasn’t well treated. We’ve been careful with ours.”

“Don’t tempt fate,” and with that, Alonzo and Jacob finished their bartering.

Shortly afterwards, the family watched as Jacob and William left their farm. They could hear William singing down the path and into the woods, the song fading as they disappeared. As the family went into the house with their new possessions, a note fell out.

“If you need help, use this spell,” and below was strange script that Alonzo could read. Alonzo showed it to Louiza and tucked it into a book. Alonzo took time to make sure Emily and Louiza could read and use the spell correctly.

⚡

WINTER CAME AND WENT. SPRING ARRIVED AND THE GARDENS were planted. The forest was dense but was still traveled by those of the woods. Many of the youths were now adults with children of their own. The community was spreading out. Some, still in the forest, some moving into the mountains, and others collecting trade goods to sell in surrounding communities.

Mid-spring reports of more of the gifted children being missing after modest adventures were brought to Alonzo and Louiza. Emily stayed close to home and only spoke to her family.

William and Jacob came back with more trade goods and a warning. They heard of hunters looking for anyone with any sort of magical ability. Jacob offered to mask the powers of Alonzo and Louiza, instead of blocking them, as he noted Louiza was pregnant again. He didn't want to mask Emily's though but showed her how to hide it herself. He had her pull out the spell he had given to her family. Jacob had Emily and her parents demonstrate they understood the spell and could use it. In the end, Jacob took the paper they had used and burned it.

Jacob and William continued to trade until evening came. William taught them all a tune that would give them the ability to temporarily distract others and warned them it wouldn't likely work more than once on any person. Jacob checked to make sure they all still knew the spell he had taught them last fall.

Emily stood tall for her age and was proud to help her parents on their little farm. As young as she was, she escorted Jacob and William to the edge of the woods. Turning back, she heard the trees groan and fold back together as the two young men passed through.

Summer came and went. Emily continued to gain strength and learned to fight from her father. Her mother was soon to deliver, and Emily wanted to protect the baby. She now understood why the women who visited the farm were hiding deep in the woods and trading with those in the mountains.

Soon, little Sarah was born. Louiza took a while to recover, and occasionally cried for her missing and now grownup boys. Sarah became a great comfort to Louiza. As Sarah grew everyone in the little family taught her. She learned her letters and math early, knew her way through the woods and remember every person she met.

Each spring and fall when the two traders stopped by. Sarah was always delighted to see them. Even as a toddler, she would know what they had before they spoke and in turn, they spoiled her with little trinkets. Emily was getting stronger and would tell them when and where to travel to avoid nearby storms. Jacob and William would trade small items for the weather reports.

Both Emily and Sarah grew strong and knew the woods, the people in it and all the gossip about the missing children. Sometimes a child or two that had been missing, staggeringly tired but healthy would show up. They would complain of a training program, and the mysterious help they got escaping. None of the children would say much about who or what helped them, just about the music they had heard.

Alonzo and Louiza would occasionally let Emily run the farm while they traveled to get supplies that Jacob and William couldn't bring. For a while, the women of the woods would come in to help, but Emily's determination to be independent and strong won out. Sarah would tag along and watch carefully, absorbing what she saw and knew. Between the two of them, they could take care of the chores while their parents were in town. Unless they had to do chores, the girls were careful to be as hidden as possible.

As careful as they all were, eventually, a stranger found them. Sarah heard him long before he reached the farm, and she and Emily ran into the woods to hide with other children. Emily and Sarah waited a long time before Sarah told them that the farm and woods were clear of strangers. At the farm, Emily and Sarah could see that someone had gone through the house, checked the barn, and walked through the garden. It was certain that someone who Sarah recognized as an unfriendly person knew that the farm was occupied and that children lived there.

Aunt Mille showed up at dusk and brought more women with her. She looked at the two girls and saw how frightened they were, so asked them to go to the woods to hide. Sarah spoke up "That won't be far enough. The man came out here was gifted and looking for talent."

Emily remembered the caves, not far from the woods. "We could try the caves. Sarah, if we hid there, do you think it would help?"

Sarah shook her head, "I don't know. Caves are weird."

Aunt Mille told the girls to pack up, and as they did, Aunt Mille wrote a simple script on the hearth, "The girls are with me, I'll be in contact." In a short order, all of them were trotting through the woods. The women left the group to get their own families to safety of the caves. Dusk was approaching and Sarah was able to let them know when she knew of someone unfriendly was near. Eventually, they reached the first caves, but Aunt Mille pressed them on. It was getting dark, and everyone held hands. The cave Aunt Mille selected had sudden turns and she told Emily to cast a light ball ahead. Emily simply pointed and a small ball of light appeared on the floor in front. It led the way to a less apparent turn.

The three of them settled down and later they could hear others settling down in other areas. Aunt Mille had snacks and a little water, so they ate and settled down for the night.

Late in the night, Sarah woke up and told Aunt Mille some of the kids in the woods had been taken. Those who had been trying to protect the little ones were taken, too. Aunt Mille asked how many, and Sarah replied "I can only count ten. Someone wants me to look."

Aunt Mille told her to sleep as much as she could and try not to wake again. Sarah looked at her, nodded and curled up between Aunt Mille and Emily as if they were sleep guards.

The next morning, Aunt Mille and the girls checked the count in the caves and found a substantial number of children and women never made it to the caves. There was nothing they could this day but wait to make sure the woods were clear. One of the women eventually told Aunt Mille that she had heard about a village where she thought the "slavers" took the children. She heard about it as if it were a story, but now believed it might have been more than that.

When the woods were clear, everyone helped gather food. All of them knew their homes were forfeit, and everyone had a plan to help those captured escape. Aunt Mille listened to each one and everyone had a different idea. Finally, Sarah looked up and said "Dad knows we're safe. He says that Emily and I should be able to help. I know where everyone is, and nobody's been killed."

Emily looked at Sarah and said, "Do you remember that spell we were given by Jacob and William?"

Aunt Mille laughed, "It actually works, but not in the way you might expect. You have to do the work and those boys do what they can, but it always goes sideways. They'll show up, but the odds of them even knowing what is happening is remote. If Emily can help me, I'll contact them and let them know what we need. The spell will have a place of its own, and it should wait until you're in trouble on your own."

And with that, everyone quietly planned and discussed what they could do. When it was finally settled, Aunt Mille said that those of the woods would know when it was time to leave. Emily and Sarah laughed, thinking of William's songs, and told Aunt Mille about it.

"Yes, it works, but it's like that spell Jacob and William gave you. It's not like a recipe or math; it just has a life of its own. I could ask them to help."

The plans were formed, and Aunt Mille sent a runner to tell William and Jacob about the latest theft. Sarah bespoke her dad and told him of their plans. He told her to stay with Aunt Mille, that he thought it would be safer. Emily agreed as she had been told how much difficult towns were becoming for anyone with talents.

People came and went, and gossip and plans did too. Supplies were gathered and Aunt Mille showed the girls how a small group could travel faster than an army. The women, Aunt Mille and the girls were all expert at gathering food from the terrain and got better since there was no longer an alternative. Aunt Mille was constantly training everyone who could fight, how to fight and telling stories of dragons, warriors, and magic spells.

One day, a young man named Michael showed up, having been sent to find Aunt Mille. He told her he was sent by a relative to help her in exchange for lessons. He hadn't heard of their plans to rescue the captured children but was willing to help. The first thing he did was re-gown the undergrowth and the trees that had been damaged in the area and to tell them to move. They were too big a group to be staying the area. He came with maps he had drawn on his travels and drew more of places about which he had only heard stories.

Aunt Mille divided up the maps and divided up the group. Certain groups were supposed to gather more people to fight and to train them, other groups were supposed to find different areas where captured people were being held. Everyone had a good grasp on keeping food in bellies from living in the woods and the wilds, so it was mostly a matter of being adept at fighting and strategy.

Emily and Sarah stayed together, refusing to part for even a meal. Even their forays for food items were done together. Aunt Mille allowed it and told them to use the spell if they were caught or captured but not until they weren't being watched. Even Aunt Mille wasn't sure that every person she had gathered to help with the effort to stop the slavers was honest.

One of the things that Emily insisted on doing was going outside to practice her fighting exercises. Sarah came along and tried to imitate the postures. Sarah also tried to keep track of people around them, sure she could prevent them from being stolen. The season had gone from early spring to near summer, and Emily knew what should be in the garden. Aunt Mille understood her curiosity and the need for food and told her that she and a couple of other women had to go with. Sarah was a closely guarded secret and only Emily and Aunt Mille knew about Sarah's talent of reading people.

They had several successful trips to the farm to selectively pick certain produce and Sarah had called it every time. Aunt Mille allowed the girls to stay together and followed them at a distance to ensure they understood their lessons in woodcraft and hiding.

Sarah learned she could be fooled, though. At the farm, with Aunt Mille nearby and several fighters on the farm, she turned and saw Emily had been grabbed and gagged by a stranger. Emily was handed off to another and the stranger started towards Sarah. Sarah got up and ran but wasn't fast enough. Sarah could feel her arms being grabbed, knew she was lifted off the ground, but didn't feel the person. The person felt like a blank to her, but nonetheless she was captured along with her sister. Others were running towards the woods towards Aunt Mille and her group. Arrows shot out and several of the slavers fell, and few made it into the woods. Emily and Sarah were taken while Aunt Mille and others kept following, reducing the numbers of their capturers.

Sarah, being held by the blank person, couldn't find Aunt Mille. Emily could see she was following Sarah, but couldn't call out, nor was Sarah able to call out. It was the first time the girls were separated.

It was a bleak night by the time they arrived at a village. The girls were kept together but Sarah was still being held by the blank person. In the end, they spent the night with the other children, many who sobbed, others who stared in blank misery.

Every morning, the girls had chores. Every afternoon, they had lessons, which hurt. Someone, somewhere, wanted certain skills developed and didn't seem to care about natural talent. It was difficult to learn something that didn't feel natural, but the children had no choice in the matter. They were being trained as a different type of warrior, using all the same spells. The slavers already knew of Sarah's talent, but Sarah had learned from her capturer and blanked herself. Little by little, in the night, Sarah and Emily taught others how to do it. It was as unnatural as an otter flying in the air, but it was important. Every child there hoped to escape using that talent, but the girls kept telling them to wait. When every slave in the camp knew how to blank themselves, the two girls agreed to call for help.

Emily and Sarah were separated, but it didn't matter. Both girls knew it was time, so they recalled the spell that asked for help. The repeated it regularly.

William stood above a small village. He could see smoke rising from cooking fires, people stirring and doing morning chores. William looked up at the mountains behind the village, took a breath, stood tall and began to sing. The song was gentle and slowly grew in volume. The villagers gathered to listen to the song. More and more gathered in the center of the village while a few ran out the far side of the village. When those escaping finally disappeared, William sang a couple more stanzas and stopped singing. He was white from exertion.

Jacob came from behind him and grasped his shoulder. "Drink this. We have got to get out of here." William drank it, cough and sputtered. "What did you put in this? It isn't out of the packet I prepared!" Jacob laughed replying, "I just added a few extra ingredients of my own... You'll see." William staggered towards the horses and fell. Jacob gave him a hand up and sent a shock of sparkles through his hand to William. William glared at him, growling, "I hate that stuff, save it for the peasants. I won't be controlled like that."

Jacob said, "Step up, man. Do you feel better? It won't change your potion a bit, and you'll feel better. They'll be after us, we have to get out of here."

The two of them rode out on horseback. As they wove through the trees Jacob put his hand up and the horses, their passengers and their trail disappeared. William chortled as he looked back and saw the trail dissipate.

"How far can we get before the trail becomes visible?" said William.

"Depends on how quiet you can be. We need to evade the villagers, so we'll be making a distraction around this hill. Get a snack and be quiet," replied Jacob.

As they got around the hill, Jacob and William got off their horses. William called out quietly a small army of squirrels ran from the woods. He whistled gently to them and stepped aside so Jacob could cast his spell them. The squirrels became multiple replicas of William and Jacob, horses, and all. William whistled and the replicas ran off in different directions.

"William, get on your horse, we have got to ride." Jacob poked William in the ribs. William and Jacob mounted their horses and rode hard and fast towards the mountains.

FINALLY, SOMEONE, SOMEWHERE WAS SINGING. EMILY AND Sarah were ready and waited for the slavers to relax, entranced. The girls slipped out and saw others disappear in different directions. Emily and Sarah, though went straight towards the music, leaving as small a trail as possible. When the music faded, Emily and Sarah were lost. They kept hiking, hoping to get far from the slavers and kept confusing their trail as much as possible.

On the first day out, Emily found a nest of fallen trees and the girls wove through them, hiding their trail. On the other side of the fallen trees, there was enough bare rock that they were able to continue to hide their trail. By reaching down, Emily could help Sarah up the steeper parts, and she cheerfully scrambled up. Emily and Sarah found a narrow crevasse and climbed in. It looked sturdy so they took their packs off and found a hidden area in which to sleep. Emily spared her own food so she could keep Sarah going. They had walked a long way, especially for Sarah's smaller but sturdy legs. They both slept soundly.

In the morning, Sarah woke Emily, and signed to her that people were approaching. They were out of the crevasse and heading up hill as fast as they could. When they reached the top of the hill, they could see a series of more hills heading into the mountains. Sarah pointed at one gap and made sure Emily knew where it was. It was more than a day away, but Emily trusted Sarah to know her business, just as Sarah knew Emily know hers.

That night, camped behind a large rock, they remembered the spell that Jacob had given the family, long ago. They were exhausted and were trying to blank themselves to hide from any slavers looking for them. Emily knew they could make the gap before noon, but they needed help. Emily cast her spell for help once again and told Sarah to wait for her turn later. Sarah looked at her, paused and nodded.

Sarah woke Emily well before dawn and showed her where they should go. Emily pointed towards another gap and Emily knew the slavers were blocking their way. So, in the dark, they changed directions and went another way. They were getting short on water, and it looked like a better place to find it, anyway. Sarah insisted on holding Emily's hand as often as possible to help blank themselves out as much as possible.

When they finally reached the first creek, it looked too foul to drink, so they continued to the next likely place. There, the water ran clear, so they filled up the water jugs, and left as little trace as possible. Any good hunter would look near a water source for their prey.

That night they spend another night in a forest, hidden in a thicket. Emily woke first, and roused Sarah. Food was getting scarce, so they had to carefully forage as they traveled. It made their trail more obvious, but there was little choice at the point. The weather was getting worse, but for some reason, it cheered them both. Emily was watching the gap get closer and closer when the clouds thickened, and air got heavy. Emily signed to Sarah to hide, as she was going to have to fight.

Sarah dodged her small body through the edge of the forest, trying stay blank while moving briskly. She found a deadfall on top of a few boulders. Hiding on the uphill side, she could still tell where everyone stood without peering. She could smell ozone gathering when a flash and an explosion shocked her. She knew Emily had been missed and was rolling farther away. Sarah crouched down, knowing Emily was going to fight. She could feel Emily grab and pull at a gathering charge and throw it right back. Suddenly several frightened and shocked adults ran into the woods, back the way they came. It was raining as one tree burned, and so Sarah ran to help Emily pick up acorns, some more roasted than others in the lightning strike.

The two snacked a little as they got away from the burning tree, counting on the rain to hide their tracks. Sarah and Emily found a thicket, and set up camp, signing each other when necessary. They were both exhausted but took the time to make sure they would stay dry through the night.

In the morning, Sarah signed to Emily that help was coming. Emily pulled a map out of the pack that her mother had given her a long time ago and looked for landmarks. She found many, including a curiously shaped tree that both Sarah and Emily had heard were directional signs. They continued on their way to the gap, having little more than acorns to eat and water to drink. They both could see the gap but were finding hiking without food exhausting.

Moving uphill, the trees became larger and the brush thinner. Emily saw a tree with a curious configuration, closely bent to the ground and then pointing up to the sky. Emily checked a map she had made years ago and saw the tree was on her map. If she followed the tree's bend she would have a longer hike, but the route looked less cluttered with fallen trees and rocks and boulders. They followed the tree's direction, gaining a view of the valley they had crossed yesterday as well as the next set of hills. Listening closely Sarah could hear water, so they kept to the trees and followed the noise to a stream. Emily filled up their container and retreated to a hidden location to clean up and drink. All they had left was acorns. Near exhaustion, they needed to find help soon.

⚡

AUNT MILLE SAT IN HER CABIN, WAITING. HER HAND WAS ON A map, and she traced a trail on the map. Many places on the map she traced a circle or two. She paused a bit, and then went over the foothills and continued up toward a mountain ridge. She looked at a young man and told him, "The girls aren't far away. They crossed the stream and are almost out of the foothills. But they are out of supplies, frightened and very weary. Could you meet them?"

"Are you sure, Aunt Mille? I wouldn't want to leave you alone," said Michael.

"If you don't, they won't be here on time. The older one doesn't know what she is, and I can't read the other girl. Don't draw attention but move quickly. Others like them are out there, but you must pick up these two. The rest will follow you, if they can. They've put less training in those kids than the two, I believe.

"Yes, Aunt Mille." And with that, the young man quickly filled a pack and hugged her goodbye.

"I'll hurry, Aunt Mille. Wait for us," he told her.

She smiled and replied "I'll try and meet you later but stop here first. I will have to help gather as many of the others as I can. "

MICHAEL STRODE THROUGH THE FAMILIAR WOODLAND. HE ONLY had a valley and a small ridge left to cross, and while the day was early, he kept thinking about those who were pursuing the girls. He did not know who was closer, he or the others. Trained, the girls would be an asset to all. If the others caught them, things could go badly for many.

Heeding Aunt Mille's warning, he regularly checked his pace. He knew the area and how treacherous it could be. A missed step could strand the girls and himself.

By mid-morning, he crested the last ridge before the foothill. He reached into his pack, pulled out a small telescope and peered downslope, hoping to find the girls. If the older girl and her sister were down there, then the animals that lived there did not know it. They were grazing, hunting, and resting according to their nature. He swept left and right, hoping to catch them going up a nearby ridge.

By mid-morning, the girls were more than tired. They had crossed a ridge, and finally found a spot to sit and rest while looking over the next leg of their journey. Emily could see a lone hiker striding towards the ridge they had just crossed. Sarah nudged Emily with a mischievous smile. The young man walked right passed them. Emily and Sarah followed him and when he came to a stop, so did they. He was patently looking for somebody, using a telescope. Sarah nudged Emily and then used her foot to send some small rocks rolling past him.

"Did you lose something?" Emily called out.

"I think somebody lost two girls and I might have found them," the young man said. Emily looked at Sarah and Sarah nodded.

"I'm about to head back to home and my teacher. Would you like to walk with me?" he asked.

"If you have something to eat, we might follow you quite a way," replied the taller girl.

"Indeed, I should have offered it already." He tucked the telescope away and pulled out a small bundle of food. "I hope this will do."

"Why thank you, we most will certainly walk with you for quite a ways." She carefully handed half the snack to the smaller girl. Both girls nibbled their snacks and all of them turned away from the mountains. The young man carefully set the pace as the Aunt Mille had told him. It had been a near thing, he had almost missed the girls altogether.

The young man introduced himself as Michael and told them they were on their way to see Aunt Mille. Both girls were relieved, and walked with good cheer.

Michael told them "We have to stop and pick up supplies. At the cabin, I helped out with tasks and chores in return for my lessons. I think we'd better load up at the cabin and take you farther. I know people are getting ready to fight those slavers. Perhaps your parents are there."

"Are we going to see our parents?" said Sarah.

"Eventually. Aunt Mille is one of the folks making sure we can stop what happened to you both. She's training people to be warriors."

"What does she teach you?" asked Emily

"To listen and speak, mostly to the ground, plants, and trees. Sometimes, they tell you what is to come or other times, what happened in the past. That's useful. I try to watch the clouds and sky, but they don't speak to me."

Sarah then asked, "Where is Aunt Mille going?"

"We won't find out here," replied Michael.

And with that, they stepped back over the ridge.

The three arrived at the cabin at dusk. Michael brought them straight into the cabin and had the girls sit down to eat and drink. Michael searched but Aunt Mille was gone. He came back to the main room and Sarah was at the fireplace holding a note.

"I believe this is for you," said Sarah.

The note told him that Aunt Mille misjudged and until things changed, to do his best to be the teacher. The girls would do the job well enough and they should hide their talents as much as possible as there was a bounty on them. He and the girls were to go to the gathering for further training.

"Did you read this?," Michael asked.

"Yes. The note is from Aunt Mille, we know her well." Sarah said. "For a time, she helped us stay out of the way of the slavers." She paused a moment.

"Emily and I followed a song, William's I think. We had an old map we followed and supplies we had saved up to run away from the slavers. The map had Aunt Mille's writing in a couple of places, so yes, I looked."

Emily walked into the room and asked, "Are we leaving in the morning? It doesn't feel right here."

"May I show you some self-defense tonight?"

"Show us," said Emily.

With that, Michael put them through several poses and motions, at a slow pace. He decided they knew more than most their age, so he showed them some advanced poses. The girls had self-defense skills but needed far more than they had. Emily, after a time asked if they could continue in the morning, as the journey had been a long one. He pushed the girls for another hour and then showed them a couple of cots. Michael told them they'd be leaving in the morning.

Michael slept next to the cabin door and dreamed of lightning strikes without rain or clouds.

When he got up, a fire was in the woodstove, and the girls finishing breakfast. Emily looked up and asked if he wanted breakfast too. Interested, Michael said yes. His breakfast was a couple of chicken eggs, some berries, and nuts.

Michael laughed and asked her, "I assume we should reimburse the neighbors?"

"Only for the eggs," replied Emily. "A day or so ago we picked up some acorns. Quite tasty, but an expensive recipe."

"How expensive?"

"Someone picked a fight. Lightning got tossed and it's hard to be accurate."

"What happened?"

"I felt uncomfortable. My mother sent me a note and a map, so when the time was right, we packed up and started hiking. A few folks we used to know took offense. They gathered for a strike, so I put one of my own near enough to send them home. And I picked up the acorns as they were nicely toasted. Why waste?"

"So, these people know who you are?"

"They didn't see me. Is it possible they might think it was you?"

"Not likely. And even if I tried to pass you off as a guy - which could happen – it would be difficult.

Emily looked up and smiled. "I might pass for another year or so. But we can move if needed."

Sarah interrupted, "There's a place with a person that I have in mind. The two who helped us aren't very far away. They need us, anyway."

They tidied the cabin, packed up foodstuff and gear for a serious hike. Walking through the woods near the neighbors, they passed a burned and blasted stump, and Michael placed a hand on it for a moment. Emily nudged Sarah and nodded towards Michael. They watched as Michael grew small saplings out of the ground near the stump. Michael smiled at the girls when he caught them watching.

Knowing there was a hard hike ahead, they picked up the pace and walked into the woods. Emily quietly pointed out short a cut when she could.

The second night out on their hike, Emily dreamed. Aunt Mille and Michael stood at a window in the front of the house. Outside the house, flowers grew and blossomed.

The fourth day, while hiking around a rocky ridge, Emily turned and asked Michael, "Did it hurt when you got your powers?"

Michael nearly broke step. After taking more steps around some rocks, he said "I was born with mine, no, not that I know. How did you come by yours?"

"Both Sarah and I were born with ours and were well trained. We learned to hide it well before we were captured. Their training was painful. Every chance we got we found a way to store some food or clothing so we could later escape. Months later, we heard someone singing not far from the village and knew it was time. So, we left."

After they got around a rocky ridge, Michael told Emily and Sarah to stand behind a knoll while he peered through binoculars over the ridge. Far below them, he could see two figures followed by a pack mule. Michael carefully crawled back and asked the girls as quietly as possible, "Do you think anyone is following you? I see two people and a mule. It's not a common area."

Sarah looked at him and silently nodded her head. Then she looked Emily and pointed two fingers and then made more gestures. Emily whispered, "Not bounty hunters."

Michael took lead and they crossed down into a small valley and found enough exposed rock to backtrack to another ridge. Crossing the stones was one careful step after another, to avoid a sliding or rolling rock that would make them easy to follow. They finally crossed the ridge and went down the other side.

Not far below them was a rockslide that came near a well-worn path through the mountains. They would have to find a way around it to get through to the path. Step by step they picked their way from the rockslide towards the path. At one point, Michael roped his waist and had Emily and Sarah hold onto the rope as they walked behind him to keep them from sliding or falling. As they approached the path, the footing got easier, becoming a grassy approach that would show their footsteps for hours. They back tracked to an area of broken trees and walked from one log to another until they reached the path.

The path was fairly level and they made good time down the mountainside. Forest grew around them and they finally stepped off of the path. The forest soon hid the path and hills as they searched for a place to camp for the night. Looking up at the sky, Emily saw a trace of smoke spiraling into the sky. She nudged Michael and said, "Can we check these folks out and see if we can join them?"

Michael looked at Emily. Emily gestured to Sarah who nodded, smiled and said, "Watch them, though. They have power and are pretty rowdy."

Michael paused and sniffed. He couldn't smell the smoke, but he could see it. So, he made a shush gesture and motioned the girls to follow him. They walked through the woods and circled around to the downwind side of the fire. Michael turned to the girls and gesture for them to get as low as possible and to wait for him. Michael carefully stepped towards the campsite and laid behind a fallen tree to listen to a couple of low voices speaking near the fire.

"William, I can't believe they tried to capture us despite of the song. Did we get paid?" said a bass voice.

"Just the portion they paid ahead of time and the horses that we traded for the pack mules and the supplies. Did you get your grimoire back?" said a baritone voice.

Bass said "Yes, I had to turn it into a handkerchief to get it out but it's safe enough for now. It's pretty heavy for a handkerchief and it's about to turn into a book again. May as well have it handy if I need it."

The baritone voice said "How are we doing on supplies? Do we have enough to skip the next place? Or should we head in and stay put a few days?"

Bass voice said "We don't have a lot of anything but leg power. Too bad we had to let those horses go. We can go to town easily enough but skipping to the next one might have dire consequences for our belts. They'd have to be seriously tightened."

"Well, we can see if we can make a few dollars. Maybe we could just have a pleasant stay and quietly leave at our own convenience. It would be nice."

Michael could smell meat roasting and his mouth watered. He crawled to the end of the fallen tree and peeked around the it. He could do nothing but sit behind the stump and wish for dinner. He felt a slight poke from a finger and there sat Emily and Sarah, grinning a bit. Emily put her nose into the air with an exaggerated sniff posture. Michael motioned to them to be as still as possible, and they all continued to listen.

"How many grouse do we have tonight?" said baritone. "Twelve. They should be ready in a few minutes. How about dried supplies, do we have any-thing?"

"A few things. I have enough for a few more days and that's it. We're going to be just able to make it. At least the packs will be light," replied Bass.

"Well, I'll serve this up. Here are yours and mine. Enjoy!"

Michael, Emily, and Sarah sat in the woods, listening to a couple of men chewing and drinking with as little noise as possible. Finally, there was the noise of cleaning up and storing cooking gear and feet walking into a tent. Bass and Baritone grumbled at each other, about who ate more than the other and what would available tomorrow. Michael and the girls listened for a long time until Michael made another wait motion. Michael crawled through the brush and disappeared.

Emily and Sarah waited for a long time, hearing only their own breathing while they crouched behind the stump. After a while, they crept quietly into the woods and circled the campsite, wanting a better view. Finally, they found a deadfall clump that was loose enough for them to wriggle through to get where they thought Michael had gone. Peering through the branches, Emily saw two pairs of feet in front of a fallen log. She was sure both pairs were Michael's and the voices softly talking were Michael's and Bass. She could get no closer, so she thought of fog, which crept into the campsite and collected thickly.

Emily signaled Sarah to wait. Sarah signaled to Emily to be wary of magicians. Emily crept further towards where she thought Michael was sitting. She pulled out a knife and gripped it edge away from her person. She peered until she heard movement. Tracking the movement, she waited until it got closer and closer to the tent. She stood, found Michael, cut the ropes on his hands and feet. Suddenly there were five Michaels each diving into the tent. The voice of Bass yelped, and familiar fellow flew back out the door. Michael followed with more rope and tied the fellow up again. He saw Emily and told her, "Watch him, he's really sneaky."

Sarah walked into camp, looked at the tied-up young man and pointed at him. "I know you. Is your grimoire safe? The multiplication won't fool me." The fellow looked shocked.

Sarah stood next to Emily who sat down and peered at the tied -up man. She laughed as she as she asked the fellow, "You look familiar. Don't I know you?"

The fellow said in a rather deep Bass voice "Sarah, you know who I am! Cut me loose so we all can out of here!.."

She laughed at the man, pulsed the ground so everyone could read him. The man with the Bass voice yelped in protest and threw his hands out.

Emily felt a splash of a spell and repelled it. "Yeah, you looked just like a donkey, too. Hold on a second…" She reached back into her pack and pulled out some acorns. "Tell me where these came from, Wizard?"

"Oak tree?" he replied.

"Which oak tree? Can you stand up?"

He shook his head no and said, "Untie me!"

She stood up carefully and checked his ankles and wrists. The ropes were untying themselves rather slowly. She pulled a bit of rope from her pack and quickly retied his ankles and wrists together. "I'm going to turn you just a little bit so you can see something."

After positioning him she said, "See that oak tree over there. I'm going to ask that tree 'Pardon me tree, bear some acorns if you think I should untie this fellow'. You, sir, should look at the third branch on the left side and watch carefully."

As he dutifully stared the branch burst into flames. And much to his surprise, a wee tiny cloud rained the flames out.

Sarah chortled and Michael grinned.

"Well, by the beard of an Unknown Being. I guess that tree didn't agree with you. How that happened is a total mystery. Have you ever seen the like?" said Emily. "Perhaps we had better wait to untie you until the tree of the Unknown Being feels comfortable around you."

Behind her, Emily heard a couple of guys chortling. Turning she saw the real Michael and another person. The second fellow with the Baritone voice said, "Yikes! Shall we bow to the tree politely? I need advice on this."

Michael replied "I think reparations are in order. If you and your friend could slowly turn around, perhaps that would be enough to heal the tree."

As the two tied up fellows turned, Michael smiled while the tree and bark healed, and leaves grew again. By the time those two characters saw the tree, the branch was fully leafed out again.

Both fellows looked at their captors with new caution. Bass said "Nice trick. Do you have any others available for purchase or rent?"

Baritone said, "Oh yeah, purchase would be good."

Emily, Sarah, and Michael stared a moment. Michael cleared his throat and said, "Didn't know you could sell that stuff. Do you do that a lot?"

"Nope, nope, not at all. Why, what have you heard?" said Baritone.

Bass glared at baritone with great suspicion.

"Sorry sir, we just walked through the woods and smelled something cooking. Thought we could share a bit of what we have for some of what you have for dinner. Introductions aren't usually this wild. Didn't expect a show before the meal. Let's start over" said Michael.

Bass said, "I'm Jacob and this is William. And you?"

"I'm Michael, this is Sarah and Emily is… Emily, where did you go?"

"I'm checking out the tree that burned and healed. Found some more acorns. And we know those two fellows, William, and Jacob, they used to visit when times were better." Emily stepped away from the tree and walked towards Michael and Sarah.

Jacob looked at the girls and said, "Did we visit your farm and trade there?"

"You two took a while to figure that out," replied Emily, tartly.

Michael turned to Emily and said "Do you have to startle people like that? We have a lot of acorns. We've had so many acorns we're getting tired of them."

Emily shrugged.

Michael told her, "If you hold still, I can look around and see if there are any fresh edibles nearby."

Michael's eyes unfocused for a moment. He pointed into the woods and said, "Third tree in".

Emily trotted in and brought fresh apples. She shelled the acorns and put them and the fruit into dish that Michael provided. "Have you two anything to contribute."

"Well, yes, there's some grouse left, in the tent. If you untie me, I can get them for you," said Jacob.

"Mumm, grouse. Yeah, I found those in this pack. Emily can you get them?" Michael replied, pointing at the pack at his feet.

Emily reached in and Sarah grabbed her arm, saying "No". Emily took a breath and pulled out a book and set it aside. Sparkles tingled her fingers and faded away. She looked at the book quizzically and then searched further for the grouse. "Got them. Let's set up."

Michael untied both William and Jacob and sat them down. The little meal went well.

Jacob looked at Emily and said, "Could you hand me my book? It has special meaning for me."

Michael told Emily to give it to him first, so she handed it over and her fingers sparkled again. Michael's fingers sparkled too. Michael turned the book back and forth Sarah looked at Jacob and said "No!" very firmly. Michael looked at Sarah, who nodded. Michael handed the book to Jacob. Sarah touched Emily who then remembered a spell that protected property, using sparkles and how to defuse it.

Jacob then asked Emily, "Are you familiar with cats? I am. Sometimes they make good familiars, too."

Emily turned into a tan and brown cat; Michael became a large black dog. Little Sarah glared at William who chortled and said, "Well, OK, but we have business in the next township.

Emily rolled her eyes and growled "Interesting. Hmmm, let's see… Isn't this the Sweet Pea and Demon Dog spell? I can undo that."

She and Michael unfolded and stood back up just as they were before they transformed.

"Be careful what you show those girls, they are dog-gone good students. It's been fun teaching them. What do you think of her final exam?" laughed Michael.

Emily and Sarah snickered, too. Michael continued, "Where are you headed? As far as we could tell you're heading toward the township due east. Do you want some company?"

Jacob looked them over and took seconds to consider his options. "Good company is always welcome. Perhaps I had better amend my manners. William, are you good with this?"

"Yep. I've been that dog too many times to disagree. Nice to know someone that can undo that spell."

Jacob carefully tucked the book inside his coat and he and William headed into the tent. Michael, Sarah, and Emily set up camp just west of the campsite, on a knoll. Michael told the shrubbery around the two camps to whisper to him should their new friends walk away in the night.

Morning came safely enough, everyone gathering next to the campfire. Emily and Michael had found vegetables and other wild foods and came up to the main camp. William had built up the campfire and was cleaning mushrooms, tubers, and herbs. He soon had them in a skillet, which sizzled nicely. Everyone enjoyed the scent. Jacob came in from the woods with another load of birds. William put a couple in a pan and cooked them up for breakfast.

Emily looked up and asked, "Do you guys eat like this every day?"

"Well, no, finding birds is pretty easy, but mushrooms and similar stuff, I've never had the knack. Some of the greens William can find, but this is really good stuff you brought." Jacob replied.

William snorted but otherwise kept quiet.

An hour later, camp was up and gone and everyone hiking together. Michael was surprised to see Jacob carry a bigger pack than William, even though William's pack included camp gear as well as a bedroll.

Two days later Jacob and William became more at ease, especially when everyone was going to the same township. Jacob asked the name of the place but got no answer. Michael said he didn't know the name, just how to find the township. Even Sarah would smile when Jacob asked.

Michael and the girls were grateful their numbers increased by two, but

Jacob and William trudged on looking a bit worried. Sarah walked as close to Jacob and William watching them carefully. They all finally started got to the road into town, went up hill and could see their goal and hear the sounds of a market. Into town they went, finding a tavern to spend the night.

The group sat at a table in the tavern and found themselves approached by a cheerful woman who handed around news sheets for a modest price.

"Here's the latest news in the town," said the cheerful woman handing the news sheets over for the coins she requested. "If you want something posted, let the bartender know." The woman went to the next tables to continue her sales.

Sarah looked up and saw Aunt Mille farther away at a table with a group. Aunt Mille her pointed at her nose and then signaled to leave her alone.

The owner of the tavern came over, introduced himself and asked, "Need some rooms?"

Jacob and Michael looked at each other and Jacob said, "I'll pass."

"Are you sure? Twenty pence for a room."

Emily said, "I think Sarah and I would like a room. How much is it?"

The tavern owner looked at the group and said, "There are beds available with the barmaids, for ten pence."

Michael asked, "How much for the bachelor section?"

"Ten pence a bed."

"We'll look at them later, if it suits." Michael said.

They ordered a meal apiece and Emily began reading the sheet of news. Emily nudged Michael and pointed down the page. Sarah peeked, too. One line said "'Book of Magic for sale. One gold sterling per book. No refunds." Michael read further looking for the seller and didn't find one so asked the barkeep. "Where's this being sold."

The barkeep carefully pointed out the directions on the back of the news sheet. Michael pointed out the ad to Jacob and asked, "Is this familiar?"

Jacob slowly turned red while holding his fork in the midair. "Why yes, it does. William, doesn't this look familiar to you too?"

William peered and looked slightly bewildered for a moment and then said, "Oh, that fellow! What do you want to do?"

"Are they active" Jacob exhaled slowly.

"Um, they shouldn't be. I didn't do anything like that. Might want to check it out. Do I have to go with?"

"Nope. If I'm not back at midnight, you know what to do."

Jacob finished his meal and walked out the door. Sarah nudged Emily and they watched as Jacob faded away, his boots being the last to fade. Emily nudged Michael and said as softly as she could "Michael, the fade spell! Jacob just did the fade spell!"

Michael looked out could see where the heels of a pair of boots were sparkling ever so slightly as they walked away. "Hm. This is getting a bit weird. I hope we don't have to do the same later."

Everyone at the table finished the meal, William paid and said, "I'll be down here for a while."

Michael grabbed their packs. He, Sarah, and Emily found the barkeep who walked them to the maids' room. Sarah shook her head. As tidy as it was, Emily and Michael could see a faint fog on the floor.

"Huh. Could we see the private rooms?"

They went to a private room and the barkeep opened a door saying, "This is it."

Sure enough, Sarah looked a Michael shaking head. She gestured slightly to a similar fog on the floor of that room. Michael looked at the barkeep's shoes and nudged Emily. They both see a very faint stain on both shoes. Emily looked up at Michael and his tilted his head towards the stairs. Michael thanked the barkeep and told him they had to consult their friend.

Back in the tavern, they discovered William singing an old song reminiscent of a spell. It had a lot of verses and most of the patrons, including Aunt Mille looked pleased with the familiar melody. When the song ended Willian scooped up a pile of coins from the counter, grabbed his pack, and joined Michael, Emily, and Sarah. Michael glanced briefly at Aunt Mille and said to Emily, "We have got to leave. There's a 'follow me' spell singling out us."

William looked at the barkeep who flipped him a coin. "Pleasure hearing that old song", he said. William in turn flipped a few coins at Michael, Emily, and Sarah.

William paused and looked at Michael and the girls. "You three look a bit related."

Michael snorted "Who knows. So do you and Jacob. Are you two related?"

William snorted saying "Brothers" and walked a bit slower.

Michael looked about and headed up the road to see if there were any nearby stables. Emily still had the news sheet, scanning for anything that might be helpful. William leaned over and pointed out two ads for stables, and Emily showed them to Michael. They looked ahead and could see the first one advertised.

Walking up to the first one, they peered into it very carefully. The horses looked well enough and there was no hint of the fog, but Michael motioned Emily and Sarah to follow him. He waited until they went past a few more buildings and then he handed the girls their packs. Emily touched her nose so Michael would look behind him. He couldn't see anything, but Michael and William split up and left the girls, trying to distract their followers.

Three blocks away, Michael heard an owl and then another hoot. He stepped aside into the shadows and waited until Emily walked past him, with an owl on her pack. Michael waited until she reached the far end of the block and looked carefully behind her. He saw shadows following her, so he waited until the last one passed. Michael turned into a large black dog, carrying a miniature version of the pack on his back. He followed the shadows and shoulder checked and knocked each one of them over. He heard running footsteps ahead of him, and he ran to catch up. Emily was just ahead of him and the owls flying close to her. They turned a corner and then another. A stable appeared and Emily – with the owls back on her shoulders- stepped into the shadows nearby. Michael stepped into the shadows next to her.

Michael and Emily peered into the stable and couldn't see an iota of purple fog nor any other spells. He whistled softly and the horses perked up their ears and turned to look. The owls flew up to the roof to roost. Emily and Michael found the ladder and they both crawled up. The stack of hay invited them, so they crawled around to the back of the hay, dropping their packs, and settled down. Michael said as softly as possible, "Be a Sweet Pea" so she turned herself into a brown and tan cat. Michael turned himself into black dog, and as he changed he realized he needed to undo a trace spell on himself and Emily. He also did an untrace function on Sarah and William. Michael and Sarah laid down between the packs to sleep.

The next morning Emily and Michael suddenly had the urge to go to the market. At the food stands, they filled both packs and tummies with the coins William had given them. They heard William singing and found him in the center of a large group of people. When he finished, Sarah put down a hat and people cheerfully put money into it. Jacob showed up on the other side of the crowd and waved everyone over to him.

"William, that person was selling loaded books. It was a faulty spell, so I undid the spells on the books I found in town. There's a lot of annoyed customers and we've got a trace spell on us," Jacob grumped. "We need to leave town." Jacob waved his hand and checked everyone over. "William, you have a trace on you but it's pretty damaged."

"Sarah and I spent the night as owls. Saw some folks approaching our roost, so we flew off to here. In the morning we had to leave a stable as we are now. I don't know what damaged the trace spell," said William.

Michael looked at Jacob and told him, "I removed our traces. I'll put Williams on something else."

Michael concentrated and looked by the crowd and saw a beautiful brick wall. Michael walked up to it and asked William to stand next to the wall. On the top, faint purple footprints followed the wall, jumped to the ground and leading downhill towards a meadow than faded in growth.

Jacob looked twice at Michael and complimented him, "Good job. Let's get out of here."

Emily and Michael spoke at the same time saying, "We're going." Emily stopped and Michael continued, "We're going to change direction a little bit. Might see you another time but we have our own schedule to consider."

"We're heading the opposite way of those footprints," William whispered.

Michael told them they had a place to visit. "We hope to meet up with some friends and restock our packs."

Jacob pulled a fade spell on himself and William, leaving Michael, Emily, and Sarah to work their way around the crowd and head towards the far end of town. As they continued, the buildings lessened in number and became sturdier and finally became rare in the landscape. Finally, Michael pulled them off the path and asked, "Emily are you two up to being boys for a while? I think I'd prefer to be a small pony, carrying the packs."

Emily replied, "I've not done that one, but it certainly seems to be a good idea. I really want to eat. How does that work, before or after the spell?"

Michael laughed. "Let's grab a snack and then I'll do the spells."

Shortly thereafter, a pony carrying both packs and the young boys walking along its side left the thicket and continued down the road. Farms appeared around them, some big, some small. Small roads threaded their way from the main road, many to houses and outbuildings, others rolled over hills to places unknown. Eventually, the road they were on became thinner and thinner until it was just barely a trace winding through the trees. The pony kept close to their side and nudged them away from the trees.

The pony stepped in front of Emily and Sarah and blocked their path. Emily and Sarah looked ahead and there were trees on each side of the trace of the path lined up. The trees were in bloom and reached over the road as if trained to be a roof over the trail. Looking further, they saw branches laden with fruit.

The pony sat and Emily, in the boy form, removed the pack and pulled food from a pack. The pony suddenly became Michael again. "Just have a snack but don't touch the trees or their fruit unless given permission."

Michael put his cupped hands in front of his mouth and produced a warble that echoed back after a moment. He and the girls, no longer looking like boys, ate a bit of cheese, drank a bit of water, and sat on the packs. They were telling each other tall tales when a tall thin man walked through the arch the trees made.

"Welcome Michael, it's been a while. Have you brought students?"

"They've passed more than a few tests already. There are people on our trail," said Michael.

"My name is Ulric. Who's on your trail?"

Emily spoke up "Technically, a group that creates a variety of warriors. We wanted to escape, and somebody gave us the means to do so, including a map. Michael found us."

Michael put out his hand and told the girls, "We have to let him look. Just hold your hand like mine and it will be quick. If it gets uncomfortable, just remember what I taught you."

Ulrich reached out and put one hand above Sarah's hand. She felt her hand warm up slightly before Ulrich pulled back his. "You're a truth seeker. It's very rare, and we have need of such."

Emily put her hand out and Ulrich did the same to her. Emily's hand warmed and began to burn slightly. Ulrich snatched his hand away quickly and watched a glowing ball form below her hand. As the ball began to drift towards Ulrich, Emily simply reached out and pulled it back into herself.

Ulrich and Michael started laughing. "Well, I guess she'd better stay with you, Michael. She's going to be needed on site. Sarah can go with another group, where she will be needed." Ulrich still laughing followed with "You all pass. We have a place for you to stay and there will be a meal shortly."

They passed through the trees and into an open area surrounded by tightly meshed trees, then a couple of stables, followed by homes and bigger buildings. They finally entered through a gate finding a mansion of stone and rock with little lights around it. As they entered the building, Emily saw the trees passing fruit to a child with a small cart. When the cart was full, a man came over and helped the child with the cart.

They took their possessions upstairs to adjoining rooms and were greeted on the stairs by Ulrich. He brought them to a large dining room. William and Jacob sat at a small table gossiping away with strange looking folks. Michael touched Ulrich and nodded at Jacob. "Who is that fellow?"

Ulrich replied, "He and his brother are traders as well as other things. We've been waiting for you."

Ulrich took Michael, Emily, and Sarah to a large table. The platters were loaded, and plates were set out for them. The others at the table looked up and greeted them briefly before attending to business and gossiping in between bites. Michael found the center of the table rotated about and they all easily served themselves. They listened to idle chatter around them and heard other people were looking forward to a well-known singer.

Michael handed Emily and Sarah a token and showed them his token as well. The bright coin had a single word pressed into it. Michael said, "You'll have to hold the coin tightly and say the word before the music begins". He grasped the token with his left hand and told them they should do the same. After a few minutes more, someone waked onto a small stage, and sparkles flew up and showered down on a small spot. William appeared in the spot and took a bow. He began to sing, acapella, a lovely tune full of adventure and mystery.

Michael, Emily, and Sarah spoke a single word and could see magic weaving throughout the audience. Some people seemed to sit or stand a bit taller, others looked like could run a marathon. Others more looked nearly hypnotized and some seemed to glow.

Soon the magic faded, and William's song came to an end. William bowed and stepped back behind curtains. Jacob stood, applauded and rest of the audience woke up as if they had been in a trance. They, too, stood and applauded while Jacob slipped away.

The three left as well, to the foyer where they met Jacob and William. Jacob gestured them to an atrium with alcoves and benches between shrubs and other plants. Jacob said, "I saw what you did in there."

"We saw what you did, too," Michael replied. "I'm going to assume we need to be ready."

William laughed and asked Emily "Can you do a demon dog?"

"He's waiting for me. You know how it is, puppies like to play but there isn't always time."

Jacob interrupted. "There's someone waiting for Sarah, who can help her develop her skills. They should meet up shortly, but I have a different idea for Michael and Emily. Tomorrow you two can meet friends. You might want to check out fighting forms tonight, on you own. William and I have more arrangements to make. It seems there are groups who are following all of us.

"Can we get any help?" asked Michael.

Jacob smirked a bit and motioned for the others to follow him. Jacob opened a door in the wall, and everyone walked down a long corridor. The sound of jocularity came from the end of the hall. Jacob opened the door and when everyone peeked in they saw child sized warriors, joking and teasing while they ate and drank merrily. Each one of them appeared to be nearly identical to all the others.

William greeted them, "Sprites! How's the party? Is there anything you need?"

One sprite stood up while the others came to a stop. The sprite replied "We are having a grand time! Is there a deadline for the upcoming activities?"

"Two weeks, two months, maybe less. There will be activity near here before then. We have a minimum of three groups headed our way. It might be a good idea to do some exercises tomorrow just in case we were followed. There's courtyard set up for you and another group. We're going to the mountains tomorrow to set up for watchers as well as some defense. Be sure to communicate with Jacob and I while we are gone.

"Yes, sir!" the sprite replied, and returned to his meal and drinking while the rest returned to the celebration.

Aunt Mille walked into the room from behind and asked, "Jacob, is Sarah with you? I've been looking for her."

"Yes, Sarah is right here."

Sarah's face lit up and she greeted Aunt Mille with a hug.

"She's fine, and Ulrich passed her. She's not quite battle ready, so she'll need to be placed carefully. And Emily and Sarah's parents will be a part of the action," said the sprite that had earlier greeted them.

Emily gave Sarah a hug and watched Aunt Mille and Sarah walk into the room with the sprites. The two of them sat down and began to joke and tease the sprites. After the sprites were sufficiently merry, Aunt Mille and Sarah left the room, Sarah followed Aunt Mille down the hall and outside to a large barn. Inside two horses were packed up with supplies for Sarah and Aunt Mille. After mounting, the two of them went down the road and out to the woods.

Soon enough dusk approached. The woods darkened the road and Sarah had qualms about it. Aunt Mille noticed every time Sarah got nervous and took a moment to pull aside and hug her.

"It's going to be fine, wait and see. Your sister is in good hands, and you will meet some people who will take care of you, too," Aunt Mille would reassure her.

Finally, they pulled onto a smaller track. After a while, Sarah could see small fires here and there. As they approached, the fires would go out. When they came up to a camp, Aunt Mille made an owl sound. Another owl sound came from farther out. Aunt Mille called out like a night jar, and another owl called back. Aunt Mille motioned Sarah to follow her and they went towards the second owl.

The two of them were ducking branches and guiding their horses through trees that barely had enough room between them for the two horses. Finally, a man came out of the dark and motioned to them to follow him. He mounted his own horse, and they found a clean track through the woods. After an exhausting ride for Sarah, she saw another fire. People were waiting around it, talking very quietly.

Sarah saw her father, smiled, and looked further to see her mother. Delighted, she hugged her father and ran to her mother and hugged her as well.

"We'll sleep here tonight. Tomorrow we are going to ride to a safer place. There's something going on there and we'll ask to help out," Aunt Mille told her.

"Glad to have you back, Sarah. Your sister is well?" asked her mother.

"Yes, we ran into Jacob and William, and they didn't recognize us. I'm not sure they know who we are now. They'll find out for sure soon, though."

Both parents laughed. "We've met Jacob and William and asked them to watch for you. They may not have recognized you as you both have grown so much," Alonzo chuckled.

"It's dark and you've traveled and long way. We have a spot for both of you set up next to ours. Set up your tent and we'll have a great meal waiting for you. We do need to keep the noise down, though," said Louiza.

Later that night, Sarah looked up at the stars and listened. The stars were calming and steady, and she could feel the entire group in the encampment. Most of them were pleased for one reason or another, some were exhausted and others asleep but not yet dreaming. Usually, Sarah would sense only one person at a time, but this seemed natural to her, too. There was no sense of her sister at all, but she had really expected it. Maybe later, when they go closer, she might find her.

With that thought, Sarah crawled into her bed, smiling herself to sleep.

Days later, Sarah was busy learning all kids of bird calls and other animal sounds used to communicate over long distances. Her horse was getting a workout, training to obey during stressful conditions without hesitation. It was crucial for everyone's survival that they work as a group and Sarah knew she was doing well.

Louiza and Alonzo would put their horses through the same paces with Sarah's horse and later other people would join them. It seemed a game to Sarah until she remembered the people from whom she escaped. One night, she had to ask about it

"Are those slavers coming after us?"

Alonzo replied, "Those slavers are part of a group that wants to enslave more than just us. If we get a chance, we'll stop them. If we must, we will run away or escape them. There's more of us, now, and we are organized. We also understand the talent they want to use far better than they do."

Louiza smiled, "We have others gathering to help us out on several fronts. It's surprising how many people don't like it when their friends, neighbors or family members are kidnapped. I'm very hopeful we can put a stop to this kind of thing."

"When will I see Emily?"

"She has her job to do. As do William and Jacob, they know we have to have someone like her. Aunt Mille sent Michael to make sure both of you end up in places where people could and would watch over you and since you both have talent, I'm sure that both of you will be helpful. We all have a job to do in this business," Alonzo interjected.

"I can't sense Emily right now. It's the first time. It faded out on the way here, but she seemed to fine."

"Let us know if you can sense her. It will be important for us to know where she might be so we can direct activity away from her or send her where she would be helpful. Michael knows he's supposed to stay with her, but we also know that might not be possible," Alonzo replied.

"I know that. I'm pretty sure she'll be OK. She got both of us to safety and Michael showed up not only to help us, but he fed us, too."

"Well, it's night and you need to sleep. We all need to sleep. So, close your eyes and rest."

And Sarah had barely closed her eyes when she fell asleep. Her body had made the decision some time ago.

The next days and weeks were spent in learning to coordinate with groups of people in an attack, a retreat or hiding. Sarah continued to learn all manners of long-distance communication with sound, fire, light and by twisting vegetation, bending a bough in a certain manner and more. She was told there would be a lot of distractions and she needed to learn this so she could help out and take care of herself when needed.

They regularly moved camp, so Sarah helped out. She was eating well and getter much stronger than she had ever been. She learned to run swiftly and for long distances while carrying a pack. Every now and again she would hear a strange thought from far away, a powerful being, that wasn't hostile. She ignored it as much as possible, but the being was becoming interested in her and was now asking questions or merely greet her in the morning or check on her in the evening.

"Good morning," she'd hear while walking to breakfast.

"Do you see the rain clouds heading your way?" was a regular query.

"There are game animals to the west," the being told her when hunting and meals had become scant.

The last one she had to tell her father, Alonzo. He passed it on to the hunters, and turned to Sarah and asked, "Is it a wizard or something like that?"

Sarah replied, "No, it's not human. It flies. It's very big. And it likes being home very much. It just wants to talk to me."

"Maybe it's a dragon. Sometimes they get chatty, but they also like to test people. Don't be rude but avoid talking to it as much as possible. They usually know more than you'd think about what's going on around you, but the less you say to it, the more options you have later. Besides, sometimes wizards are looking for talent to use and don't play fair. Can you block it?"

"Well, it's not very pushy, just rather curious. I'll try," said Sarah.

"Just be sure to tell your mother or I if there's a problem," said Alonzo. "If you're done with your chores, you have a little time before the midday meal. It's sunny out, you should have a little fun, but stay close."

Sarah always stayed close. She had learned to sense a blank person but still feared being caught. Every day, she helped her parents add to their stores of food, mushrooms, herbs, wound treatments and so forth. She helped with hunting and trapping food occasionally but preferred to stay close to camp. Today she just climbed one tree after another until she went up the highest tree to see as far as she could in every direction. Looking in each directions, she saw mountains, valleys, smoke from towns, birds and more. Looking in each direction she saw a grassland with waving grass. She looked again and the grass was moving in one section.

She climbed down, found her father, and told him. Having time, he went up the tree and looked. He came back down and held her hand while they went to camp and found Aunt Mille.

"You didn't try to sense anyone, did you?"

"No."

Aunt Mille looked at Sarah and asked her, "Can you watch through a dragon or something else large? It might be a good way to look at something."

"Unless the dragon doesn't like it," Sarah responded. She thought for a moment and told her "Why don't I try to watch through an eagle? There's some in the area."

Aunt Mille and her dad nodded, and Sarah closed her eyes. She found an eagle and discovered she could see what the eagle saw. She waited and the eagle saw the grass moving. The eagle flew over it, expecting prey but saw people walking in the very long grass. The eagle had no interest, so Emily pulled away and opened her eyes.

"It's people walking through the long grass. The eagle wasn't interested, so that's all I know."

Alonzo told Aunt Mille, "They could be here in a day or so. We should probably move."

"Dad, wait and let me try something." Sarah merely let herself sense them.

"They've left someplace in a hurry and are seeking refuge. I think some of them are warriors and others are trying to keep up with them. They have no place to go."

Aunt Mille and Alonzo went through the camp explaining to groups, Alonzo saying; "We have a fair number of persons walking towards us through the grass. They seem to be refugees, but we need to confirm that. If we break up into different groups, Aunt Mille and I can investigate them and disperse them though out our groups – even if they are slave hunters."

It took little time to organize everyone, pack up and move different groups to different camps. A night and a day passed when Alonzo and his group came back with more people. They were tired and been on the move for a long time, having crossed the grasslands from the mountains and were grateful to be among other people. The new group previously lived in the woods so finding places in the grass to settle was new. Aunt Mille spoke to each group, explaining how to use the grass, find game and leave a minimal trail. Alonzo did his best to make sure they were hiding their trails.

That night, after making sure everyone was settled in the camp and fed, the fires were covered for the night banking a few coals for morning. Many of the original encampment quietly spread out through the woods to watch for anyone following their guests.

Sarah's skills were immediately announced to the new group. Alonzo pulled her aside and said, "Pay attention if you notice more people approaching. Watch for someone moving from group to group and let me know."

Aunt Mille walked into the conversation, "I worked with the sprite warriors, and they should be heading this way soon. I was supposed to meet them at the pass, but I doubt I can get there in time."

"Is there any way they can get here without help?" Alonzo asked.

"They are familiar with the mountain passes, including the dragons that inhabit them. Can Emily let the dragons know they are coming here?'

Sarah looked at her and smiled. "The dragon checks on me nightly. What

I know, the dragon will know."

Aunt Mille nodded and said, "Good."

That night was quiet enough and those who stood watch traded with others in the morning. The morning campfires were pretty quiet, but the new-comers expressed their gratitude repeatedly. One person named Cleve spoke quietly about their escape and travels.

"I and many others left our village after several hunters told us about chil-dren being stolen from nearby places. We knew we were being followed and most of us had little woodcraft. Those who did tried to hide our trail. We fi-nally found a mountain pass and entered a cavern that went from one side of the mountains and out the other side. As far as we know, nobody managed to follow us through the cavern. We tried to keep our trails hidden and watch our children carefully."

Cleve explained in more detail about their escape and trip, and how grate-ful they all were at being taken into a larger group.

As Sarah listened to the story, she looked at the adults in the morning light and realized they were thinner than their children. She paused and patiently waited to feel something from either the adults or the children. After some time, she finally felt a child relax and then knew the story was very true. The children had spent nights in fear, hiding where the adults directed them. The adults had gone hungry to keep the children fed.

And she knew the child was someone who could block the thoughts of others and spent a long time doing so. The child had judged their encampment as safe.

Later in the day, she told her father this. He smiled and told her they still needed to watch for several reasons including the possibility of the child having been fooled. Parents want to protect their children and often do so by not tell-ing their children the truth. So, Sarah continued to watch and listen, trying to keep her talent safe.

One night, the being that pestered Sarah finally sent her a dream. She saw the new people from a dragon's view – before they reached the cavern. He sent them a dream of the cavern repeatedly before they reached and entered it. It was the dragon's cavern and he watched over them as they passed him. The slavers had tried to follow but the dragon took offense. That group's bones decorated both the interior and exterior of that particular entrance. Thankfully, the Sarah wasn't seeing any of the bones of those who had offended him, but he merely stated the fact in the dream.

Sarah told her father of the dream as well. Her father had been talking to person after person and the stories were very similar, apart from what happened to the slavers.

Next time Sarah slept, the dragon sent a different dream. There were others in a similar difficulty, and he wanted to send them to her. Many were warriors, some who brought families, all plagued by the slaver's entrapment attempts.

She told her father of the dreams and he asked her if the dragon could talk to him instead of her. No sooner said than done and the dragon's voice was in his head. Alonzo knew how many people of the next group warriors were, how well equipped they were and when they would reach the valley. Alonzo, smart enough to know what to do, asked the dragon the best place to defeat the enemy. The dragon had no information but told him the people coming his way were seasoned warriors able to find several defensible places. The next group was large enough for more than one encampment.

Soon enough, the new people were divided between encampments, with trained runners between them. The warriors went from camp to camp to train others to fight. Some encampments had those with magic about them and the warriors worked with them so they could help during a battle. Each group had been stopped by and met the dragon, who had thoroughly checked them, and he had introduced himself. The dragon had told them they would need to defend the area of grassland, woods, and mountains.

The dragon had also told them he expected to be there when there was a need, too. This encouraged everyone.

Each encampment found food enough where they were, and were able to grow in fitness and health, and the warriors continued to train each group to fight. The smaller children needed a place to hide, and each group found a different spot for their children when fighting broke out.

It was peaceful enough for now, but nobody expected it to last long. Too many of them had escaped or knew someone who had, from the slavers.

⚡

Jacob motioned to Michael and Emily. They all walked

back into the hall and the door closed behind them. They could all hear the sprites partying as they walked away. They went back through the atrium into the main part of the hall, bidding each other goodnight, going their separate ways.

In the morning Michael and Emily followed their noses to the same dining room. They were waved through to a table where Jacob and William sat. Morning meal items were spread on the table, and everyone helped themselves to what was on the rotating platter in the middle. After a while, Jacob excused himself, telling them to wait for him. The other diners from the previous night were present, many sitting straight and tall, others looking cheerfully determined. A few of them still seem to glow with less intensity and others paid attention to what was happening all around them.

Jacob came back and waved to them from the door. They went down the hallway, past the sprites' dining area, and out another door. In an open area before them was row after row of sprites, performing perfectly synchronized exercises. Aunt Mille and others were performing similar exercises with another large group. Jacob and William saluted the sprites and the humans, who paused and saluted back. Jacob stood at ease and the warriors continued their exercises.

Jacob led them to a private room and shut the door. He handed Michael a map and told he should seek help in the circled area. Michael and Emily took the map over to a table and unrolled it. Emily found the encircled area and pointed to it without touching the map. Michael held his hand over it and said, "Watchers are near there. We are going to need supplies."

Jacob handed Michael a slip of paper and told him to visit the sprites for the needed supplies. "By the way, you and Emily have a month to get to the encampments. Soon enough, there will be enemy warriors trying to come though those passes. We'll be able to hold the main road and protect the surrounding population for a while. We'll have to find a way to guard or close those mountain passes before you come back."

An hour later, Michael and Emily were on a narrow side road leading up a path that went up into the mountains. By noon, they were overlooking a meeting of mountain ranges. Looking below Michael briefly pointed to a rocky spot mid-way down a mountain. "Emily, can you spot the growing gravel well above that stream. That's part of a weak spot. Look up a little further and find the chimney formation filled with ice and snow. Up above, there's a cloud. If you can put enough ice into that chimney formation, you can break up the mountainside and fill up the gap. We have to pass that area first, but I wanted to make sure you knew what it looked like from a distance."

Emily narrowed her eyes. After a moment, she pulled a partial Sweet Pea spell, and her eyes could see farther into the shadows.

Michael watched her and said, "Good job. But you might want to use a hawk instead."

Emily looked about and saw eagles and a hawk riding the currents. She thought a moment and could see the area through hawk eyes. She coaxed the hawk around the area and after she was through, she found an area in the stream loaded with fish and suitable game. She let go of her gentle hold on the hawk.

Michael touched her shoulder and handed her a chewy snack and then took a bite of his. He gestured with his head, and they began to hike across the rocky spot. They were quiet and stepped carefully. Several times Michael stopped and pointed to a weak spot in front of them and a few behind them. They were both exhausted when they reached the other side, but Michael touched her shoulder again and indicated they should push on. It was nearly evening when they stopped. There were fewer trees, large rocks and shrubs. After setting up camp they were worn out, so they used more of their dried stores instead cooking. It was also very cold, so they set up a tent. Shortly after, they rolled up in their sleeping gear.

In the morning, Emily woke up and smelled hot food. She rolled up her sleeping gear and attached it to her pack. Michael's pack was already set up, except for the cooking gear and tent. When she went out, Michael pointed at her plate and said, "Time's running short. Gotta get going."

In a brief time, Emily had her breakfast, broke down the tent, and packed up the miscellaneous items. Michael told her, "We have to go right now."

They both slung on their packs, and Emily followed Michael. She noticed he was doubling back on last night's trail. When Michael came to a stop, he pointed behind them and muttered some words. Emily watched as their footprints disappeared, and plants that had been damaged by their passing healed and hid more of their trail.

They reached a spot where they could see the chimney formation. Michael looked across the gap between mountain ranges. He looked up and saw clear sky and a lake on the far side. He told Emily, "Pay attention. Do you see the first crevasse?" Emily looked at the sky above and put her hands out. She gathered energy out of the mountain skies and pulled it together. A bolt of lightning shot and hit three places around the crevasse.

Michael and Emily heard the rocks and stone cracking and a rumble as the whole thing shifted. Michael exclaimed "Let's go, that sounds a lot bigger than I expected."

They both scrambled back into the woods and found a knoll to stand on. They looked back and see nothing but dust and snow rolling into the gap. The lake on the far side spilled water into the gap and began to freeze.

Michael merely said, "Well, the next one will take a while to get to."

Hours later, Michael and Emily were at the second gap. There was snow on both sides, and they searched for a safe place to stand and retreat. Michael found it first and waited for Emily to speak up. Finally, she showed him an area with a solid path, with high mountain shrubs and trees around. Michael looked at it and said, "I chose a different spot, but I think I can use the growth to protect us as we leave."

They got to the path and Emily looked over and found a snowpack that would work nicely. She froze the rocks below and melted the snowpack into the rocks. When they felt a slight rumble in the rocks below they ran down to the trees and scrub. There was a crash behind them. Michael grabbed Emily and pulled her into a cavern. After the noise settled down, they looked out seeing the trees that had fallen and stones that had rolled in front of the cavern. They could still see a place to exit at the top, but the stones didn't appear stable.

They both stepped farther into the cavern and found a niche where they felt safe. It was mid-day, so they made a meal out of dried fruit and dried smoked meat. Once they had finished, Michael pulled out a water again and told Emily to go easy on it. "We'll have to get more soon. We're going to camp here."

Michael and Emily rolled out their gear, set up camp for the night and were soon asleep. In the morning, they ate more of the dried items. Their water was getting low. Michael looked out the entrance and decided to check the cavern for another exit and potable water.

They were soon on their way towards the darkness in the cavern. As they walked, Michael told Emily to put out her hands. He reached into the air and pulled out a blue flame and placed it in her hand. "Is this familiar?" he asked.

"No," Emily replied. "But I can duplicate it." She handed the glowing ball back to Michael. She reached out into the air and an orange one formed in her hand.

"That's a flame of a different color," Michael chuckled. "We need to be really quiet." Then Michael spoke in her head instead of out loud. "Beware of old magic."

Emily and Michael both reduced the flames as much as possible and trod lightly as they wound through the cavern. After a while, they could see shining objects on the ground. Emily reached out to pick one up and Michael stayed her hand. "Old magic is ahead. Don't touch anything. Step carefully. Sometimes such things are traps, other times they are a test. Stay close. I'm going to hang on to your pack and you are going to be quiet, including where you put your feet." Emily nodded and paid attention to how Michael silenced her shoes, garments, and gear. It seemed easy to do and she wondered why she had never been taught such simple things.

They stepped around the shining objects and could see they were silver coins. Farther down the cavern they saw more shining objects and realized they appeared to be gold coins. Michael spoke inside Emily's head and said, "Stop. Look ahead and stare blankly a moment. What do you see?"

Emily unfocused her eyes, reduced her flame to a small sparkle in her palm and tucked it behind her.

"Good," said Michael. "Look ahead and stare blankly for a moment. What do you see?"

Slowly Emily's eyes adjusted to the dark and ahead she could see small glowing slits. She waited a little a longer and realized they were floating midway up in a large cave off to one side. Michael spoke in her head, "You see it? That's a dragon. If we had picked up any of the coins, we'd be dead. I'm going to greet the dragon. He may ask you questions but be sure he will know your every thought."

Michael cleared his throat.

A sibilant voice came from the cave. "What have we here? A teacher and a student, with different magic arts working together. Could you possibly explain the blockage in front of my cave?"

"Well, there's an invasion on the way, different groups, from different areas. More people like she and I will be in trouble in we don't block off one more mountain pass." Michael said.

The dragon came a little farther forward towards the entrance of the cavern, his eyes growing bigger and glowing brighter as he advanced. "Yes, they've been gathering below for some time. Right now, they are counting survivors. It'll be days or more before they can move from here to there. It'll probably take the two of you some time to get through the blocked entrance let alone to your destination."

The dragon looked at Emily and said, "Little one, I can tell your powers have changed from their original purpose. Who did this to you and forced your adaptation?"

Emily looked at Michael and he nodded his head. Emily hesitated a moment and replied, "Many of us were simply captured and had training forced on us. It wasn't comfortable, to say the least, but I did work hard at it. I escaped. I'm here out of desperation. I wouldn't mind stopping those slavers from using people like me."

The dragon looked at her and whispered, "Close enough." The silence made the hair on Emily's arms stand up on end. Her fingers began to tingle, and she held out her hand and showed Michael a small glowing ball sparkling and glowing above her hand.

The dragon spoke again, "I beg your pardon. You certainly are more than I expected. I've been waiting for someone like you. I know another dragon at the next pass and I'm sure she'd stop those of ill will rather than letting them pass through. We can get you to your family. They are living in the grasslands near the next probable battle ground. Did Jacob bring William?"

"Yes!" exclaimed both Michael and Emily. Michael added "They are traveling somewhere near here, making some preparations for defense, if needed."

"Ah, yes. Good thing William has an interesting singing voice. Heard it recently, in different places weaving several spells. That's how I knew you were coming. I'd better get you two to where Jacob and William will find their forces. Bella and I will watch the passes. When it is time, we will block most of the passes and when the battle is done, unblock them. You will need to get ready for the first battle, let alone the others. The slavers aren't likely to give up easily."

Michael grasped Emily's shoulder and pulled her well back and away from the cavern. The dragon chuckled a bit. "No need. The best way out is behind me. I'll put my head down and you two can grab your gear and secure your-selves just in front of my shoulders. Let's not waste time."

Moments later, Michael and Emily were seated neatly on the dragon. "By the way, my name is Angus."

The dragon turned around and went through the cave, around a couple of corners and stepped out onto a ledge. Moments later, Michael and Emily were hanging onto the leather gear with their eyes closed. Emily squealed a couple of times and then kept quiet. They could feel the surge of the wind as they flew higher and higher.

Sometime later, Angus called out "I'm going to slow down and land. You can peek a bit."

Michael laughed, so Emily opened one eye. They were skimming a forest where the branches seemed to be waving them on. Soon, they came to the end of the forest and to the grasslands. The dragon landed and said, "Sarah says I'm to drop you off here. Your father is nearby and will take you to camp."

Michael said as formally as he could, "We thank you heartily for the trans-portation and the news."

Emily looked ahead and saw another dragon in flight and below sprites and humans just on the far end of the forest. They were both in formation, looked up and saluted the dragon.

Later that night, when all was quiet, Aunt Mille, Sarah, Jacob and William stopped by their tent. "I thanked Angus and Bella for bringing you. Thank you for blocking the passes."

William spoke, "When the battle begins there will be a lot of noise you won't hear with your ears. None the less the noise will powerful for those sen-sitive to it. We have something for both of you. Don't lose it, as you won't be able to tolerate otherwise."

Aunt Mille handed both of them a knitted cap. "Tie it up under your chin now. It will also be cold. The hat will block dragon screams as well as blind your trail. Pack everything up early in the morning as we won't be stay-ing. I'm sure Emily can arrange the snow. The sprites love it and move quickly on and through it. Could you manage at least knee high?" Aunt Mil-lie held her hand just above her knee to make sure Emily wouldn't use her shorter stature as a guide.

Emily looked at Michael and saw she was the only one not wearing a cap. Putting it on, she made sure it covered her ears. Michael nodded at her, so Emily reached up and felt the cold from far above coming down. She brought some moisture from the mountains to meet the cold and it began to snow. She kept it going until drifts built up. She closed her eyes and could feel the snowdrifts piling up.

Jacob asked, "Can you take it to the mansion where you stayed? Or perhaps beyond it?" Emily kept her eyes closed and as time passed, she felt the snow piling up far away, around that beautiful house, in the gardens and beyond. Jacob stood behind her and Emily could feel him throwing a spell into the snow.

Michael grabbed her shoulder and said quietly, "That's enough. You're chilled through and you're shaking."

Emily opened her eyes and saw several warriors, both big and small, lined up with hot food and beverages. Both the human and sprite warriors seemed unusually cheerful, and after they handed out everything they ran out into the snow. They were building snow walls around the encampment and throwing snowballs at each other. Aunt Mille and Sarah were cheerfully directing the snowballs from one group to the other. Both groups of warriors were entirely silent, but Emily could feel their gaiety.

After their meal, Jacob told them he'd wake them up in the morning. They would need to break camp and the spell attached to their hats would cover their tracks.

Everyone headed back to their own tents and turned down the lights inside. Michael and Emily had rolled out their sleeping bags and found them floating above the ground cloth. Amazingly, the snow didn't cause the tent sag at all. Michael looked at Emily and said, "Jacob and William are doing a great job. Everyone here has a lot to defend."

Emily discovered her sleeping bag was quite warm and swiftly fell asleep. Michael used a spell of his own to scan a bit of the surrounding woods and found nobody but the sprites and human warriors, the dragons and the four of them in it. He fell asleep moments later.

The next morning, Aunt Mille, William, the warriors and Angus and Bella were gone. Jacob had his pack on his shoulders and signaled to Michael and Emily to get ready to move. As they were packing up, all three could hear a loud dragon roar from above. Jacob told them, "Ignore it and keep those caps on your head. We have to get moving right now."

Jacob directed them to a rocky ridge off one side of the forest and told them to defend that area – as long as possible – and make sure there were as few injuries on both sides as possible. "The other side is made up of kidnapped and enslaved people. They have no idea what is happening. Misdirect them. You will know who the enemy is and who isn't as Aunt Mille and Sarah spelled our side. William, Aunt Mille and I will be fighting and will depend on you to do what we ask, if we ask. Sarah will be here in a moment, and she'll help out. Aunt Mille will tell her when it is time to leave, so when Sarah says go, go, and don't stop."

A short time later, they were trotting through the snowy woods with Sarah. Emily glanced back and there were no footprints behind them. They kept pace through the woods and came out of the woods. Jacob pointed to a large mound and told them to go behind it. Jacob ran back to the dragons. William, on Bella, waved to Jacob who was greeted by Angus. The dragons swept up into the air with William and Jacob and flew over the forest.

Michael and Emily stood behind the rocky ridge. Far too quickly, people came running through the woods towards them, most of them rather dazed, others crazed with anger pushing the dazed ones ahead of them. Michael tells Emily to get the angry and screaming ones separated from the rest.

Emily puts out one hand and one sheet of lightning leapt up from the ground. The dazed people stumbled forward. Michael waited until the lightning dropped. He spotted the others picking themselves up, so he tells Emily to try chase them into the woods. Emily sends balls of lightning to chase the others into the woods. The small balls seem to zip towards the enemy and tag them with a crackle. The slavers staggered back to try and grab as many of their buddies as they can and drag them out. The balls floated slowly towards them and the slavers, who were nearly hysterical, sped up their escape towards the woods. The ones left on the ground, laid there, dazed.

The dazed ones picked themselves up and stagger towards Michael and Emily. Michael grew vines up through the snow and tangled their legs. Held fast, the slaves pulled out knives and cut away the vines. Michael gestures towards Emily, so she takes a turn. As they escape the vines, Emily forces them to circle back to the forest with more lightning, both ball lightning and strikes from above that barely scraped the snow. As they get to the forest, both forces join together and head back towards Michael and Emily. Emily repeats the lightning a few more times before the slavers and the dazed slaves stepped farther into the forest.

Michael says, "They're going to try to flank us. I'm going to block the on the right side, you catch them on the left." Trees shoot up out of the ground and block the path of the slavers and slaves, which created a fence armed with prickly thorns. Michael grows more just on the far edge to force them further back.

Emily was busy blocking them and was startled when the slavers start running into the lightning. They screamed briefly and the ones behind them drop and roll away. Shocked, Emily took a quick breath before she repeats it. She saw more father off to the left and sends lightning bolts to shock the ground. Most of them run back and try to follow the others on the right.

Emily takes a breath and sees Michael grow enough trees to create a trap, capturing many of them while Emily chases most of the rest into Michael's trap. Some of them have weapons and try to hack their way out but Michael's spell keeps the trees growing and entwining them.

Emily hears strange noise from far away. She finds a hawk and uses it to see William and Jacob, on dragons, chasing another group of slavers farther away. She calls out to Michael "They are chasing the rest of them away." Emily hears Sarah, as if she's far away "Leave quickly," and tells Michael.

Michael looks at his trap and finishes it off. The slavers are trying to hack through the thorns Michael grew, a very thick barrier. "These folks will be busy with their wounds, later on. And very itchy, most of them with puffy eyes. We've got another task coming up." They pick up their gear and they take circuitous route. More than once Emily and Michael look back and defend their trail or distract the few followers remaining. Eventually, neither of them sees anyone on their backtrail.

After a few exhausting hours, they arrive at the stone mansion from behind. The gardens were now confusing and the trees surrounding it seemed menacing. Finally, they find a wall by bumping into it. They feel along the wall until Michael finds the right place. Michael pushes vigorously on a spot, which opens the door. He and Emily enter. It's much warmer inside than outside, a welcome feeling after camping outside. Michael steps aside and releases what now appears to be a solid oak door. Now inside the solid rock building with a fire in the fireplace, several huge tables some covered with maps. There are a telescopes, bookcases, chairs, and cupboards. On one wall are plaques and medals, a few that appeared to be military awards. Hallways and doors are spread out everywhere. Michael said, "We are staying in this room. Don't stray, magical beings of all kinds can enforce privacy and respect." Michael also points out a sign above a door declaring "Sentry Tower. Bespelled Against Unauthorized Entry."

They both put their packs behind the door and look out a window facing the road they had traveled. Two dragons with riders were flying over the forest looking as if they were screaming. Michael picked up a telescope and could see people running away from the road, mostly back towards the mountains. He could see sprites smiting those who hesitate to send them to follow the rest of their company. Michael hands another telescope to Emily and said "Do you know how to adjust? Rotate this part and it will change how far you can see."

Emily sees the sprites running about. She couldn't tell what they were doing but did see people on horses entering the woods and chasing those on foot back out of the woods. She thought she saw William on a horse following the rest, and it looked like he was singing, directing the ground troops. She tilted the telescope upwards and has to adjust it. Then she caught sight of two dragons who had two Jacobs as riders. Suddenly they both blurred and then dozens of dragons appeared throughout the sky. A larger dragon appeared with Aunt Mille on the far side of the woods and skimmed over the woods as if it was searching for something.

Every now and then one of the Jacob and dragon team would swoop down and appear to scream with a little fire. Emily looked towards the far end of the woods and saw Aunt Mille, her dragon, and people on horseback chasing other beings farther away from the woods and back up the road. She put the telescope back and found Michael standing in front of a large book. He looked up and motioned her over. Emily walked over to look at the book.

Michael pointed at the page, and it was describing the battle in neat writing. It logged deaths, prisoners, survivors, and those needing medical attention. Michael pointed farther back, and the book showed their entry in the Sentry Tower. Nearby was a map showing small dots moving about. There were two large black dots moving back up the road, farther and farther. Some of the smaller dots broke apart and ran back towards the woods with large dots continuing to pursue the rest back up the road.

Michael and Emily returned to the book. Those needing medical attention were being transported in wagons by the sprites as well as some men and women. Another detail had been assigned to those who passed on.

Michael went to the backpacks and brought them to the table. He pulled some food from his pack and put enough food on the table for at least four or five people. He and Emily ate a simple meal and as they were cleaning up after themselves, they heard a soft roar. Looking out the window, they saw a shadow flying over the snow and past the window. Another one followed. Shortly afterward, there was a bump at the door and William and Jacob entered. William was holding his arm and Jacob helped him to a chair. Jacob opened a cupboard and Michael went to William and checked his arm. "Emily, bring my pack over. I have some stuff that works well on this type of wound," said Michael.

Emily brought the pack over and Jacob came over to watch curiously. Michael broke open a package and spilled some powdered substance onto a cloth. William had been bleeding, so Michael cleaned his wounds and applied the powder, and tied a cloth over the wounds. The bleeding stopped.

Michael looked at Jacob and asked, "Does he have any more wounds?"

"You got the most dangerous one. I'd check his head and I wouldn't be surprised if he hadn't strained his vocal cords. He saved a lot of lives on both sides."

Michael checked William's eyes and found the pupil to be the same size. Then inspected his scalp and found it to be undamaged. "Michael," rasped William, "Jacob was joking about the head injury. But I could something for my throat. Singing and sending orders to troops is tough and dry work."

Jacob started laughing. William growled slightly. Jacob laughed some more. "Michael should give you some of his tea. We'll check your head later and see if you can eat." Jacob turned to Michael and told him, "All the silent noise he hears makes his ears ring, especially when he sends the replies. The dragons also need attention."

Michael put away the package and pulled out another. He handed it to Emily saying, "Make sure you use a big mug but use this powder in the water. Heat it up and wait until it changes color, then give it to William. If William protests, let Jacob or I know."

Jacob took Michael to the dragons, and they complained of assorted scrapes. Michael had to pat his poultice on the wounds and let them dry. Angus and Bella both relaxed into a sleep position. Jacob asked Michael, "How long will they be out?"

"They aren't out. I believe they are just very tired and are resting." Michael cleared his throat and said, "We saw you on the map, flying everywhere. If you have a better place for them, this would be a good time to get them there."

"Bella and Angus, there's a better place to rest. There's a hidden room that the dragons can use on this side of my home." Jacob swept his hand up in a dramatic gesture. Angus opened an eye, and he could see a huge door drop forming an entry. Bella sniffed and she and Angus ambled over to peer inside. Bella turned back, raised and eye ridge and went inside. Angus followed and from inside he rumbled out "Most suitable."

Jacob told them, "Tap the panel next to the entryway to close or open the door. There's a back entrance, too."

The door rose and closed. Jacob and Michael went back inside.

William was sitting up and he and Emily had a meal ready. It was near nightfall, so Jacob pointed down a hallway and said, "There are bedrooms plenty enough for more than this little group."

The next morning, everyone smelled food cooking. Michael and Emily met in the hallway and went back to the main room. William greeted them while Jacob was working over a book. Jacob looked up, pointed, and said, "Breakfast is down that way." Jacob continued to flip through the pages making notes on a separate sheet.

The three of them followed their noses to a room filled with food laden tables, sprites, and other warriors. Some were serving and others were eating. William waved at a few and called out a greeting or two. As people finished, they picked up their plates and took them to a table where others took the plates to be cleaned. William, Michael and Emily picked up their meals and found a table. People would walk by and salute them. When they were finished, they went back to check on Angus and Bella. Inside the huge room, they found it led to a cavern. They found the two dragons with a local news sheet. Angus saw them and pointed, "There are some spare news sheets right over there."

A small table with three chairs appeared. One the table, the news sheets clearly said, "Rebel Warriors Crushed the Slavery Kingdom". William pointed to his name and Jacob's. "No, not really, is my name in public news sheets, too? There's Jacob's name, Michael and Sarah's too."

"No," laughed Bella. "This particular news sheet is only for our side. It dissolves when the slavers touch it. A pretty simple spell."

Jacob walked in asked, "Angus, when is Aunt Mille due?" Angus looked inward and said, "She's almost done sorting out the wounded and sending others to rescue those with magic from slave encampments farther away. She'll be here today."

A little later, at Angus's direction, Emily looked out one of the windows and saw Aunt Mille and Sarah riding horses out of the forest. Emily ran out to greet them and hug her sister. Aunt Mille took the horses to the stables and the girls helped put away the gear while chattering about their parents. Aunt Mille told Sarah they were on their way which filled both of the girls with good cheer and hope.

On their way back to the mansion, Sarah and Emily looked up and saw Aunt Mille and Michael looking out the window. Emily reached out and took away the snow. The sun brightened and flowers began to grow as Michael and Aunt Mille laughed and waved the girls inside. Emily looked out the window and could see her parents riding up the road. Running back outside, both Emily and Sarah helped their parents settle the horses and brought them to the mansion. Contented, they all walked into the main room to settle near Aunt Mille and Michael in front of the fireplace.

Jacob walked in and looked at the group. "I have good news and bad news. Your previous homes have been destroyed and there are still bounties on all of us. You are all welcome to stay here."